SHADOW OF THE ROSE

Whilst working on research for her boss, Liza accidentally overhears a sinister conversation. When her brother's name is mentioned, she naturally begins to ask questions — but, instead of answers, she finds herself engulfed in a maze of superstition involving witches and a deserted house on the moor. Right then, falling hopelessly in love with her boss, Anton Demegar, was something Liza could have done without — especially when it seemed that he was at the root of all the mystery.

DEE WYATT

◆

SHADOW OF THE ROSE

Complete and Unabridged

LINFORD
Leicester

First published in Great Britain

First Linford Edition
published 1998

British Library CIP Data

Wyatt, Dee
  Shadow of the rose.—Large print ed.—
Linford romance library
1. Love stories
2. Large type books
I. Title
823.9'14 [F]

ISBN 0–7089–5363–8

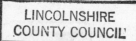
Published by
F. A. Thorpe (Publishing) Ltd.
Anstey, Leicestershire

Set by Words & Graphics Ltd.
Anstey, Leicestershire
Printed and bound in Great Britain by
T. J. International Ltd., Padstow, Cornwall

This book is printed on acid-free paper

1

Liza's foot pressed down on the accelerator as she overtook the groaning lorry in the inside lane. There was no need to rush, she wasn't expected at Lovell House until early evening and, moving back into the inside lane, she kept to a steady sixty-five as the motorway cut through the craggy range of hills that formed the Pennines.

The clouds reminded her of puffs of cotton-wool as the wind, growing stronger by the minute, scudded them across the sky. It was the first sunny day for ages — perhaps it was a good omen. The motorway was almost deserted now and Liza drummed her fingers on the wheel, humming along to the cassette playing softly from the dashboard.

'Well, I still think you're crazy going so far away, Liza! For all you know this Anton Demegar could be another Yorkshire Ripper!'

Liza smiled a little as she heard Megan's words again in her head. Megan always was a worrier, and their farewell glass of wine last night had been shadowed with her friend's doubt and scepticism. But perhaps she was right! Perhaps all her friends were right!

She was a little crazy uprooting herself like this and throwing her lot in with a man she'd never even met. She glanced briefly at the digital clock on the panel — it was not yet two o'clock and the sign loomed to tell her that the next exit was for Daneshaw. Well, crazy or not, it was too late now.

The narrow road swept across the peat-brown sweep of the moor, reminding Liza of a pale ribbon that wound away into the distance and, a little further on, a sign told her she'd seven more miles to go. Only seven more miles and, after driving for nearly four hours, she felt like a wreck. Her new boss was expecting a refined academic and not something the cat had dragged in, so she pulled over on to the verge to freshen up.

Liza dug around in her shoulder-bag for her make-up purse, scrutinising herself critically in the small round mirror of her compact. Not bad when she was only a couple of months from her twenty-eight birthday. Her eyes, as she took off the tinted driving glasses, were still her best feature — everybody said so. Wild and dark, like a gypsy. A wanton, Johnnie had always called her. A bleak shadow momentarily crossed their dark depths as she thought of Johnnie — he'd said a lot of things, and more fool her for believing him!

With a shake of her long dark hair, Liza shrugged him out of her mind. It was no use thinking of Johnnie now, he was gone and that was the end of it and, opening the car door, she stepped out on to the moor. The air felt fresh and clean and the wind, strong now in this exposed bleakness, caught her hair, whipping it back from her face and almost taking her breath.

Her heart thrilled as she looked around. This was her home ground. She and her brother Charlie had been born less than ten miles from here at Tock's Beck and, reaching for a scarf from the glove compartment and tying it around her head, Liza walked a few paces along the verge and up a narrow track. It felt good to be out of the car at last and her eyes swept along the low, brooding sweep of Pendle Hill, docile now in the late afternoon, then following its length to the claw-like jut of Brindle's Leap.

She laughed softly to herself as she wandered on, remembering her brother and how he used to plague her to death with his stories of witches. She pulled her woollen jacket more tightly around her slim shoulders, feeling the wind bluster as though in play until, inevitably, her thoughts strayed to Anton Demegar and wondering what he would be like to work for.

Liza pursed her lips. It was unlike her to be impulsive like this; to take a job without a formal interview. But Professor Williams had been assurance enough. Her own contact with her new employer had been scanty to say the least, either through correspondence or the telephone, and she had no idea what he looked like. His voice had been attractive though, it had held a warm quality that somehow fascinated her. And the lucrative salary he'd suggested was an offer she couldn't refuse.

The wind carried the sound of a dog's bark across the moor, interrupting her thoughts and causing her to turn her gaze across the moor towards the sound. Liza shaded her eyes against the sun's bright glare, looking over to Brindle's Leap. The dog yelped excitedly as it covered the ground, black and ghost-like against the skyline.

A man was giving chase and, even at that distance, Liza sensed his anger. The sun emphasised the redness of his hair and Liza could hear his angry, fragmented shouts as the dog bolted towards the summit of Brindle's Leap. The red-headed man gave chase for a while, covering several yards of ground before he was forced to give up. He stood watching the animal until it was lost to sight, then he turned abruptly, striding away to vanish from her view.

Liza shivered again, making her way back to the warm familiarity of the car. She sat perfectly still for a few moments, looking out across the moor and wondering what lay in store for her now that she'd almost reached her destination.

Why was she suddenly so afraid? What would she find waiting for her at Lovell House? She sighed, no doubt she'd find out soon enough and, turning on the ignition, she set off again along the road that would take her into Daneshaw.

It was market day and the little town was busy. Liza edged her way along the cobbled main street as it rose steeply to the war memorial at the top. The market traders were pitched half-way up, and the rows of crimplene skirts and fruit and vegetable stalls spilled out on to the pavement from the crowded square.

Turning left as instructed at the war memorial, Liza drove for a further four miles before turning into the drive at Lovell House, pulling up in a paved courtyard and glancing somewhat nervously at the ivy-festooned facade of her new — albeit temporary — home.

She got out, opening the boot and lifting out her bulging case before she rang the bell. A deep throaty bark of a dog came from somewhere round the back of the house and, seconds later, a man's gruff command, '*Down, William! Stop your noise*!' The door was opened by a short, roly-poly woman, sixtyish, with grey-streaked hair and a chuckling, squeeze-box voice.

'Come in, come in, you must be Mr Demegar's new assistant . . . '

Liza had barely managed to say

that yes she was, before, in next to no time, she found herself seated in a pleasant sitting-room, sipping tea and surrounded by a mountain of buttered scones — feeling that she'd known Anton Demegar's housekeeper all her life instead of just a few short minutes.

The woman told her her name was Milly, and as she bustled around Liza like a queen bee, she gave Liza a breathless non-stop account of Mr Demegar's likes and dislike's, do's and don't's and assured her that Mr Demegar would see her just as soon as she'd had her tea.

When the woman had finally gone, Liza looked around. The room was pleasant and tastefully furnished. A log fire had been lit and above it, on the mantleshelf, was a photograph of a small boy. Liza moved closer to look and found herself grinning at the fair unkempt hair and the shiny impish face. At the end of the room was a picture window, heavily curtained in green velvet and looped back now to reveal a wide sweep of a well-kept garden.

Liza moved along the room to look out. A dog, a black labrador, was scooping his big paws into the soft earth and making a terrible mess on the path, while over by the greenhouse, a big-boned scrawny man was digging at a vegetable patch. His grumbling voice reached Liza's ears as, not surprisingly, he rebuked the dog, then turned his head towards the door as Milly's voice called out to him.

'Norman! Leave that for now and take Miss Bancroft's case up to her room, there's a good lad.'

Liza grinned again as the 'good lad' threw down his fork and ambled towards the house, the dog following eagerly, its tail wagging in anticipation of more exciting things to come. She turned back into the room hoping Mr Demegar wouldn't keep her waiting much longer because now she was feeling grubby and travel-worn, longing to take a shower and change her clothes.

Then something caught her eye. In a corner and by itself on a small table was a photograph of a young woman. There was something about it that drew Liza closer for another look and, peering down, she saw the face of a young woman about the same age as herself.

The face was beautiful in a fragile way and Liza was drawn to the eyes, eyes which held depths she found hard to fathom. There was a hint of spoilt petulance about the full mouth, and she sensed an air of helplessness and frailty about her. Somehow, this gave Liza a strong feeling of the girl's vulnerability and fear, causing her to feel a little sorry for her. Moving away, Liza wondered vaguely who the girl could be. Was she, perhaps, Mrs Demegar . . . ?

'Miss Bancroft?'

Liza spun round at the sound of the voice. Somehow, she'd expected him to be older, but he looked no more than thirty-five at the most. He was standing rather sardonically in the doorway, his dark eyes narrowed against the shaft of sunlight which beamed through the window, catching him in its glare.

'Mr Demegar?' Liza took a small step forward, holding out her hand to receive his clasp of greeting as he strode across the room to meet her. 'I'm pleased to meet you at last.'

'May I offer you a drink? And, do please, sit down.' He indicated with a sweep of his hand for Liza to seat herself on one of the chairs as he moved easily towards the drinks trolley. 'What is it to be? Sherry? Campari? Scotch?'

Liza sat down, recognising at once the low attractive timbre of his voice. 'Sherry would be nice, thank you.'

She watched with interest as he poured some into two glasses. He was singularly good-looking and his manner, no less than his voice, held a sort of careless charm that could be quite devastating. Liza sensed an inate

11

virility as she observed him, handing her a glass and then moving away to ease his tall frame into a chair facing her. His eyes, dark-fringed, intelligent and penetrating swept her from head to toe.

'Welcome to Lovell House, Miss Bancroft — and to our . . . working relationship.'

Liza smiled her thanks and took a sip of the sherry, its relaxing warmth creeping almost instantaneously into her bones. She looked candidly across at her new employer. His head was inclined slightly to one side, still sizing her up, and the light from the window threw a shadowed slant across the hard line of his cheekbone. His scrutiny was beginning to make her feel uncomfortable and she was relieved when, at last, he spoke again.

'Professor Williams has sent me a glowing account of your researches into medieval history, Miss Bancroft. I was particularly impressed by your paper on Richard the Third.'

'Thank you — I'm glad you found it of interest.'

'Oh, I did — very interesting. I gather you feel that Richard had a raw deal — that he was innocent of the crimes history has accused him of.'

'Yes, I do, though it's impossible to prove, of course. But I haven't found any proof against him either.' Liza smiled wryly. 'The Tudors covered their tracks pretty well.'

He was still eyeing her with interest, but now a ghost of a smile touched his mouth. 'Have I taken on a Yorkist? A white rose?'

Liza smiled too. 'I'm afraid you have, Mr Demegar. Do you mind?'

'Not at all.'

Their eyes held each other appraisingly for a few fleeting moments, each sizing the other up. Then, his voice, very quietly but with a flash of humour, said, 'Anton.'

Liza held his gaze squarely, that ghost of a smile still playing around his lips. 'Sorry?'

'Shall we drop the 'Mr Demegar'? Most people call me Anton.'

Liza turned her dark gypsy eyes to his, meeting his challenge as he got up from his chair. 'Very well . . . Anton . . . When would you like me to start on your manuscript?'

Anton Demegar grinned, his good humour evident in his eyes. 'Well, certainly not today, Miss Bancroft, you must be shattered after your journey. And I have to go out tomorrow, and I may even be in Paris on Monday so Tuesday looks to be the nearest we can come to grips with the Plantagenets. Still, it'll give you time to settle in, to get yourself acclimatised to our northern hills.'

Liza nodded, then murmured, 'I'm quite accustomed to the northern hills, Mr Dem — ' she corrected herself hurriedly, ' — Anton — I was born here. And, by the way, my name is Liza.'

'Well, Liza . . . ' he grinned, 'Perhaps, later when you've had a little rest,

14

you'll allow me to show you around. Do you like horses?' At Liza's nod he went on, 'Would you like a ride before dinner? Or have you travelled enough for one day?'

'No, I'm not tired, and I'd love to ride. The problem is I haven't brought my riding clothes. Most of my stuff is in store until I have my own place again.'

'That's no problem, you can borrow Elizabeth's gear. You look about the same size.'

'Elizabeth?'

'My sister.'

'Won't she mind?'

'No, I shouldn't think so. Anyway, she's not here — she's way on holiday.'

Liza stood up, putting her glass down on to the table and smiling, 'In that case, if you're quite sure, I'd love a ride.'

'Good, I'll get Milly to root them out.' Anton Demegar moved across to stand beside her. He was tall, well over six feet and, even though Liza herself was taller than most women, she felt overshadowed by the powerful charisma of the man.

She listened as he told her of the things he'd show her on the moor, his deep attractive voice compelling, betraying his inate masculinity. 'We could ride over to Pendle if you like — if it's not too far for you.'

Liza assured him that it wasn't as he led her to the door. She'd ridden over that particular stretch many times before with her brother and looked forward to doing it again with Anton Demegar. Who knows, perhaps she could show him a thing or two herself!

'I'll see you in an hour,' she murmured as she made her way up the wide staircase.

By the time Liza came out of the shower, Milly had already laid out Anton's sister's riding clothes on the bed. Everything fitted like a glove except the jacket, it was much too tight, so Liz discarded it for a warm red sweater and, when she

16

went downstairs a little while later, she found Anton already waiting for her with two saddled bays.

Her cue had arrived. The play was about to begin.

2

Anton and Liza set off across the moor at a steady trot. Everywhere was ablaze with heather and now, in late August, the bracken was touched with the first muted gold of autumn. The wind was still brisk but invigorating, and Liza delighted in the way the sun chased the shadows across the slopes, filling the deep valleys with light.

Anton looked at her with a challenging smile. 'Up to a gallop?'

Liza laughed, taking him on. 'Why not? I'll beat you to the beck at Deep Cutting.'

'You're on.'

The mare's silky mane streamed like a pennant as Liza urged her on, and by the time they reached the crags of the Cutting, neck and neck with Anton, Liza wasn't sure which one of them had enjoyed it more. They reined to a stop,

18

laughing and breathless, and as Anton helped her dismount she could hear the exhilaration in his voice. 'Terrific. How about a breather?'

They walked a few yards towards a low dry-stone wall and Liza leaned against it while Anton tethered the horses to a withered shrub. After a moment, as they gazed across the spectacular scenery spreading around them, Anton pointed over to his right.

'See the rise there?' Liza nodded as she followed his direction and Anton went on, 'Just beyond it is Richard's favourite home, Middleham. Of course, it's little more than a shell now.'

'Are we so near?'

'As the crow flies, yes.' He turned to watch her expression, grinning slightly at her wide-eyed gaze. 'He may even have ridden along here. He often did, you know, when he wasn't away fighting either for his brother or for his throne.'

Liza squinted her eyes against the sun, looking towards the rise and her imagination taking over and musing. 'I can almost see him. It fills me with a sort of . . . I don't know . . . A sort of awe, I suppose. I wonder if he ever rode here with his Lady Anne.'

'I doubt it. Wasn't she on the delicate side?'

'So they say.'

He reached into his pocket and pulled out a bar of chocolate, 'Hungry?'

'Mmm . . . Starving . . . '

He broke the bar in two and they munched the chocolate in silence for a while, until Liza asked, 'Where has your sister gone for her holiday?'

Was it her imagination or was it the sunlight? Did Anton's eyes narrow slightly at her question? Then he turned and held her in an expression that Liza found almost frightening as he answered, 'She's in Bermuda.'

Her disquietude faded. 'Bermuda? How lovely. Is she there for the summer?'

Anton stared out across the moor. He didn't answer her directly and he was so quiet that Liza began to think perhaps he hadn't heard her. Then, very softly, he said, 'No, only for a few weeks.'

'When are you expecting her back?'

His tone was crisp. 'I don't know.'

She was getting a feeling that the subject of his sister was unwelcome, taboo, and that he really didn't want to talk about her at all. He moved away towards the beck, stooping low to pick up a few pebbles and toss them one by one into the water.

Liza stood silently by the wall, wondering what on earth could be making him so suddenly tense, and a little puzzled by his change in manner. Then he turned abruptly, dazzling her with that sudden smile. 'Come here, Liza, look at the fish.'

She moved to his side, gazing down into the clear water of the beck and watching the flashing silver gleam of the fish as they darted like tiny arrows. She knelt down, splashing her fingers in the cold clear water — remembering her brother again and how they used to fish these becks when they were little.

'Damn!'

She glanced quickly towards Anton, hearing his muttered curse. He'd cut his finger on a sharp stone and blood was beginning to seep onto his palm.

'Oh, let me see.' Liza reached into her pocket for a tissue and dabbed at the blood, then she wrapped another one around his finger. 'That's not too tight, is it?' She looked anxiously up into his face only to find his dark eyes on her, holding her in an amused expression.

'It's perfect, thank you, Nurse Bancroft.'

A little embarrassed at his open scrutiny, Liza jumped up quickly and went back to stand by the horses, glancing at her watch. 'Isn't it time we made a move? The light will be gone soon.'

Anton grinned again, getting up and walking over to take hold of the reins. 'I suppose so,' he said quietly. 'It's such a pity, though. I could stay on these moors forever — especially in such pleasant company.'

They moved away and Liza felt oddly flattered by his last remark. She knew what he meant about the moors, though, she'd always loved them too.

That night Liza fell asleep almost as soon as her head touched the pillow and, after breakfast next morning, she put her head around the kitchen door to find Milly sitting by the Aga, truculently slicing the heads off a colander of carrots.

'Is Mr Demegar anywhere around, Milly?' she asked.

'No, he left early. He said he wouldn't be back until later this afternoon. Did you want him for anything special?'

'No, he told me he had to go out today and I hoped to catch him before he left, that's all. Did he leave any messages for me?'

Milly walked over to the sink and ran the colander under the cold water tap. 'No, he didn't say anything.'

'In that case, I thought I'd go into Daneshaw — find my way around the shops. Do you need anything while I'm there?'

Milly's flushed face creased in thought for a moment, then she said, 'Would you bring me some stamps, two first class? And can you pick up my antibiotics from Wilson's the chemist? My chest's playing me up again.'

'Right, two stamps it is, and your antibiotics.'

She picked up the prescription from the table as directed by Milly's red, dripping hand, then paused, turning back as she caught the harrassed look on the housekeeper's face. 'I don't have to go into Daneshaw, you know, Milly,' she said. 'I could always stay here and help you out.'

'No, pet,' Milly answered wheezily, turning her attention back to the carrots. 'You'd only be in my way.'

Liza turned towards the door. 'Well, if you're absolutely sure. I thought I might do a bit of sight-seeing so I'll probably have my lunch in Daneshaw.'

Milly grunted. 'There aren't all that many sights to see in Daneshaw, luv, although the church is worth a visit, I suppose.'

Liza laughed, 'Right, Milly, the church it is.'

Liza parked behind the town hall and set off down the incline towards the main street. Daneshaw was a pretty town, its stone houses scattered haphazardly up from the main square. The single main street virtually sliced the town in half, cutting through the centre and curving steeply until it reached the river at the bottom.

The fast-moving river Dane, from which the town got its name, was spanned by an old pack bridge, but farther on, as Liza observed, a wider, modern road bridge now took most of the traffic. More efficient perhaps, she mused, but not half so attractive.

Retracing her steps, Liza crossed over to the post office to buy Milly's stamps. She also bought a couple of view cards to send to Megan and Professor Williams and a local guide-book 'Daneshaw, and its Origins'. Then, picking up Milly's antibiotics from the chemist three doors away, she weaved through a cluster of narrow side streets until she reached the church.

St Lawrence's church was not one of the oldest in the land, nor was it all that interesting in architecture. According to the guide-book, the main church was seven miles away at Corston, and St Lawrence's had been built as a daughter chapelry in the first half of the eighteenth century.

Liza pushed open the heavy oak doors at the main entrance and paused at the statue to the martyred saint. He stood just inside the flag-floored chantry, on a plinth by the font, and as Liza looked at him he seemed to stare back at her rather reproachfully.

She had the place to herself and as she walked down the centre isle she read the names on the family pews.

There were Astleys and Thorntons, Parkers and Crosses, and even a Bancroft or two, but she paused as she came across the largest and most spectacular of all.

This pew was long enough to take a large family and the whole of their household as well. A brass plaque at the head of the pew read, Demegar of Lovell House, and from the size and position of it, it was patently obvious that the Demegars must have been the local bigwigs.

Liza moved on through a zig-zag of pews and aisles until she reached the Lady chapel. Here she stopped, enchanted by the enormous display of flowers that had been arranged in readiness for tomorrow's services. It all felt so peaceful and tranquil that she just had to sit for a while and rest her aching feet.

It was so pleasant sitting there that, for a moment or two, she let her thoughts stray, thinking of her new job, her new home, and, most of all, of her strikingly handsome new boss.

Suddenly, through the quietness, came a man's voice.

'Where have you been? You're late!'

Startled, Liza turned her head but could see no-one. She was entirely alone and whoever was speaking was directing his question to someone else — someone out of her line of vision. Then her sharp ears picked up the sound of a woman's voice, answering, 'I couldn't get away!'

There was a rustling, like paper, and the man's voice came again sullenly.

'I was here ten minutes ago.'

'Did anyone see you?'

'No, there's no-one here. A girl was wandering about for a while but she's gone now. Come on, we haven't much time. Here — take this and keep it until you hear from Mike.'

Liza had no wish to eavesdrop on a lover's tryst and thought perhaps she had better move from the Lady chapel and let them know she was still there. Just as she turned to move, however, the woman's voice came again, edged with fear.

'This is too dangerous! Can't you keep it? I don't want — '

The man interrupted her roughly. 'Pull yourself together and do as you're told.'

The woman answered him breathlessly, the tremor still in her voice. 'He's back — I've seen his car, and if he sees me . . . '

The woman's tone sounded desperate and Liza leaned back against the wooden pew. This was no lover's tête-a-tête.

The man's voice, when it came again, was grim. 'For God's sake, get a grip on yourself. Leave it to Mike, he'll know what to do.' Then his voice softened. 'Don't worry, he always gets you out of it, doesn't he? He did before, remember? All you've got to do is sit tight until you hear from him — it won't be long.'

The woman murmured something Liza couldn't catch, and then he went on, 'You do trust us, don't you?'

'Yes, I have to.'

There was a pause and then the woman spoke again, this time calmer, but Liza could still hear the tautness of her nerves all the same. 'I've heard he's got someone to help him with his research. Do you think that's wise? Do you think it will be all right?'

There was another pause then Liza heard them move off together, but not before she caught his faint reply. 'How should I know? I suppose he knows what he's doing. Anyway, it'll keep his mind on other things until we need him again.'

Liza didn't move for some time after they'd gone. The palms of her hands felt damp as she gripped the arms of the pew. She sat frozen in thought, having unwittingly been an eavesdropper to a strange conversation between two people, one of whom, the woman, was so obviously frightened.

'Someone to help with his research!' Could they possibly be referring to

Anton Demegar and that someone was herself? If not, who else could it be? This was ridiculous! There could be many researchers around here. After all, wasn't there an atomic energy laboratory some miles away at Crayburn? It must surely be something to do with them.

Liza stood up, slipping her feet back into her shoes and moving slowly out of the Lady chapel. She side-stepped one of the screens to head towards the door when, suddenly, she stopped, frozen. Standing alone by the altar was a woman, and Liza had no way of knowing whether it was the same woman she had overheard talking to the man, or whether it was someone who had merely come into the church to pray.

Whoever it was, she still didn't move and Liza recognised her instantly. When the girl turned to walk away from the altar Liza had seen her face clearly, and there was no mistaking that delicate, fragile face. It was the girl in the photograph in the sitting-room at Lovell House.

One hour and a pot of strong tea later, Liza abandoned her plans to explore Daneshaw any farther and headed back to Lovell House. For the rest of the afternoon she busied herself revising her research into the Plantagenet kings of the white rose, preparing her work ready for Anton Demegar. But it was no use, her concentration lapsed and, try as she might, her thoughts strayed inevitably to the girl in the church — wondering what it was that made her so afraid.

It was about five o'clock when she heard Anton drive up to the house and, moments later, there was a knock on her door and Milly's head came around to tell her that Anton wanted to see her downstairs right away. When she went into the sitting-room he was standing by the window looking out into the garden and, hearing her approach, he turned.

'Enjoyed your day?' he asked, handing

her a glass of sherry.

Quietly Liza answered. 'It's been . . . interesting.'

'I'm glad to hear it. How interesting?'

Liza told him. She told him of her visit to the church and of her interest in the statue and the Demegar pew. He listened to her with amused attention, smiling now and again at her descriptions of insignificant things. It was when she came to the part about the overheard conversation that he changed dramatically. His eyes hardened and they scanned her face in disbelief.

He got up from his chair abruptly, moving back to the window and looking out. Liza's eyes followed him, puzzled, and a stirring of something that was close to alarm began in the pit of her stomach.

He was angry, and there was a dangerous power about him. An uncomfortable silence filled the atmosphere, making Liza more and more puzzled. Why was he reacting like this? And who was the girl in the photograph? What was his connection with her?

Liza studied him through lowered lashes. She observed his back as he stood at the window, his broad shoulders almost blocking out the light. Was he a man to be feared? Yes, indeed he could be! She could feel his domineering force from where she sat.

After a few tense moments she could no longer contain her curiosity and, keeping her voice as calm as she could, Liza indicated with a small sweep of her hand towards the photograph.

'The girl in the photograph, Anton. Who is she?'

He swung round to face her, his eyes flickering darkly. 'Why do you ask?'

'I'm curious.' Liza's tone was tinged with just enough coolness to show her interest wasn't anything personal. 'I believe I saw her this morning in the church.'

Suddenly his eyes were as cold and

as hard as flint. 'You're mistaken! The girl in the photograph is Elizabeth, my sister, and I've already told you she isn't here.'

'But — '

'I repeat! You're mistaken!'

He threw back the remainder of his sherry in a dismissive gesture. It was obvious that the matter of the girl in the church was closed as far as he was concerned, but his voice, when next he spoke, sounded decidedly rattled.

'It's almost time for dinner.'

As Liza moved to follow him from the room she glanced again at the photograph. If it wasn't the girl in church, then it was her double. How could she be on holiday in Bermuda and in the church in Daneshaw at the same time?

When Liza tore herself away from the photograph to move to the door it was to find Anton Demegar's eyes regarding her with an almost frightening intensity. He held the door for her to pass, the expression on his face defying analysis. Then, suddenly, the coldness was gone. And it faded so quickly that Liza couldn't be sure if it had been there at all.

3

Dinner had been wonderful and now it was very late. Liza was finding it extremely difficult to stifle a yawn as Anton glanced at his watch and then at her, 'More coffee?'

Liza shook her head. 'No thanks,' she smiled, 'I couldn't drink another drop. It's been very pleasant, thank you.'

'The pleasure's all mine I assure you,' Anton returned. 'In fact, I can't remember when I enjoyed myself so much.'

'Thanks,' Lisa murmured, smiling at the compliment and seeing in his glance a flicker of approval at the saffron silk pants suit she had chosen to wear.

Liza swallowed. The way he was looking at her and the seductiveness of his voice was doing strange things to her equilibrium. It was time to move, she thought.

'Well, thank you again,' she said, stirring in the chair as if to leave. 'But look at the time, all this talk about King Richard has exhausted me.'

'I'm not surprised,' he countered with a grin. 'Old Lionheart had a knack of exhausting everyone. It was his thyroid, you know — it was overactive.'

'He wasn't that bad,' Liza defended. 'And how do you know he had thyroid trouble?'

Anton chuckled. 'How else can you account for all that nervous energy? He chased around medieval Europe like a madman. He must have been an absolute pest.'

He was teasing and Liza knew it. The banter was good-humoured, but through it, Liza sensed that he admired her, respected her views. He'd listened earlier to her defence of the other Richard — the Third one — and he'd agreed that perhaps history had been more than unkind to him. And she'd learned something else over dinner. Anton had already been married.

She had learned how his wife had died in a car accident when their little son was less than a year old, and she'd listened as he told her of the way he'd picked up the pieces of his life, giving her a warm feeling of respect and admiration. And once — just once — when they'd reached across the table for the same piece of cheese, his hand had accidentally brushed against hers. Their eyes had met and she'd blushed as she realised how much she liked his touch.

Reaching for her purse now she asked, 'Will we be starting work tomorrow?'

His eyes darkened fractionally as he answered. 'Fraid not. I shall be out most of the day and by the time I get back it will be too late for any work. What will you do with yourself?'

Liza gave a small shrug of her slim shoulders. 'I'm not sure. Perhaps I'll go through some of your notes if that's all right.' Anton nodded briefly and Liza continued. 'Then, perhaps, later I'll go for a walk, take the dog up on the moors.'

His eyes lifted suddenly and Liza felt that uncomfortable jolt in her heart again. 'I'd rather you didn't do that,' he said quickly.

'Why ever not?'

'There's been some talk — some sort of trouble. Locals are saying the witches are . . . ' He broke off, laughing softly to cover his obvious embarrassment.

Lisa gave him an incredulous stare. 'You surely can't be serious?'

But she could see he was. The laugh had stilled and his face was grave as he went on. 'I don't believe all that stuff, of course, but I still think it would be advisable to stay away from the moor for a while. Take your walk somewhere else — by the river, perhaps. Even better, stay around here.'

Liza took a little time to let his words sink in before pointing out, 'But we were on the moor yesterday and they looked harmless enough then.'

'That was different, I was with you. And, besides, we were miles away from Hazlehurst.'

'Hazlehurst?'

'It's an old house where all the trouble seems to be. It's been derelict for years. It got a bad name after it was discovered that it had been used as a covern some years ago. Nobody'll buy it now and, because of its isolation and reputation, it's handy for any bunch of weirdos who need somewhere to doss. There are some there now, and that's why I'd rather you kept away when I'm not here.'

Liza studied his serious face for several minutes more before she finally accepted that he was only thinking of her safety.

'I suppose you're right,' she murmured before switching to something that had been puzzling her since her arrival. She queried, 'Anton, how did you come to choose me to do this work of yours?

41

How did you know about me?'

Liza waited as he swirled the remainder of his brandy around the glass. He swallowed it down and took the glass over to the trolley before he answered, 'An old friend told me about you.'

'Who? Professor Williams?'

'Your name came up when I was looking for an assistant. Your reputation has gone before you. I contacted you, you fitted the bill, I made you an offer, you accepted, and here you are. Satisfied?'

She wasn't, but she knew that was all he was prepared to tell her tonight so, when he reached out his hand to help her out of the chair, she accepted without further demur.

A smile flickered across his face as he looked down at her, sending an uneven thudding through her heart. 'Goodnight, Liza. Sleep well.'

He inclined his head and lifted her hand, brushing his lips on it lightly, and before Liza could say anymore,

42

he'd crossed the room and she was alone.

Lisa did sleep well, like a log in fact. She awoke next morning to the sound of subdued voices in the courtyard below her window so, slipping on a robe, she opened the curtains to another beautiful day. From the window she could see Anton already in the drive, reminding her more of a well-heeled farmer than the international airline executive she knew him to be. And even less did he look like the renowned amateur historian with a penchant for the fifteenth century.

He was standing, feet apart, by a grey, low-slung Mercedes sports car talking to Norman, his hands thrust deep into the pockets of his dark-coloured jeans. His face was hidden in the shadow of the peak of the tweed cap that covered his thick dark hair, and the cream Aran sweater seemed to enhance even more the broadness of his shoulders.

She heard his, 'See you later,

Norman,' as he climbed into the car, swinging his long legs under the low driving wheel.

Lisa showered and put on a pair of comfortable bib-trousers over a white sweatshirt, tying her heavy dark hair back with a scarlet headband. After breakfast she made her way to Anton's office, determined to come to grips with this job she was being paid to do and, as she looked around, she saw that an area had been cleared for her use. There was a desk and an electronic typewriter set neatly by the window, a small filing cabinet and, on a table by the desk, a pile of manuscripts.

It was twenty past twelve when Liza finally looked up from the manuscripts. Outside, the sun was glorious and, as she got up to look out, she could see William dozing in a pool of sunlight by the greenhouse. There wouldn't be many more days like this, she thought. Soon it would be autumn, then winter, and winter always came early and stayed late on this high ground of the Pennines. She picked a book from the shelf, taking it over to the window-seat and reading a few lines from 'The Yorkist Sunne'.

Lisa felt suddenly restless. It seemed a crime to be indoors but Anton had insisted, and she wasn't about to antagonise him this early in their association. She closed her eyes. He puzzled her. One minute he could be so amusing, so charming, and the next . . . He would change suddenly, become brooding and bitter, so much so that she could almost sense a tyrant. Liza didn't know whether she feared him or not. She knew she would never be able to ignore him, or want to get on the wrong side of him.

She opened her eyes, placing the book back on the shelf and going upstairs to her room. Lying on the bed she thought of Johnnie. It had been more than a year since their break-up and she waited for the inevitable pain to start again in her heart. She waited, but this time it didn't come. For the first time she couldn't see his face, or remember his touch. This time all she could think of were those dark penetrating eyes of Anton Demegar and the way her reflexes acted up whenever he came anywhere near.

'*LIZA!*'

In the space of a few seconds the peaceful stillness of Lovell House erupted into a pandemonium of noise, cutting through Liza's brooding concentration like a bolt of lightning.

She sat up with a start as the sound of a car's doors slammed, and William's excited barks mingled with the laughing shrieks of a small boy. Liza jumped up and ran to the window. The drive, which had been so empty and peaceful just a few moments ago, now seemed to be remarkably full of a small boy and his big black labrador.

'*Liza*!' Anton's voice came again from the hall and Liza ran quickly across the room and out on to the wide landing.

'I'm here, Anton. What is it?'

'Liza, come down. There's someone I want you to meet.'

When she went into the sitting-room some minutes later, the little boy was standing by the open french window throwing sticks for William to chase. He looked about six or seven and, as Liza entered, his intelligent little face, rosy with excitement, turned shyly to lift two wide dark eyes to hers. Those dark eyes, dark-fringed and serious, were Anton's all over again.

'Liza, this is my son, Stevie,' Anton announced. 'Stevie, this is Miss Bancroft, the lady who's come to help me with my book.'

Stevie held out a small hand in polite greeting, brushing his unruly fringe out of his eyes with the other. 'I'm pleased to meet you, Miss Bancroft,' he murmured, obviously well schooled in meeting adults. 'My Dad told me about you in the car.'

Liza smiled as she took the boy's hand. 'And I'm pleased to meet you,

Stevie, but I'd like it better if you called me Liza.'

The boy grinned shyly before turning back to his father with a pleading look in his eyes. 'May I go and play with William now, Dad?' his tone implying that his duty had been accomplished.

'Soon. I'd like you to get to know Liza a little better before you do that.'

As he spoke the phone rang from the hall and Anton excused himself to answer it, leaving Liza and Stevie alone in the sitting-room. Liza perched herself on the nearest chair, aware of two round dark eyes observing her shyly and waiting for her to make the next move. 'Milly tells me you've been at Grandma's for a few days, Stevie.'

Stevie nodded. 'I've been at Grandma's nearly three weeks — while Dad's been away. But I can't take William there, she says there's not enough room.'

'Well, he is a bit on the big side, isn't he?' Liza commented drily as the dog came lolloping through the french window to drop a stick at Stevie's feet and paw him impatiently. 'I should think he needs lots of exercise.'

'Yes, he does,' agreed Stevie, rubbing the dog's head affectionately. 'He likes it best when we go up on the moor 'cos he likes to chase rabbits, but Dad won't let met go up there now.'

His face, which had been so childlike and open, showing a bright intelligence, suddenly became masked, and Stevie seemed to look older than he was. There was a sort of hardening in his small bearing, a kind of withdrawal, and as he bent over William's head, Liza could see something else in his dark eyes — she could see anger, and she sensed fear there, too.

Anton's return dispersed the uneasy feeling. Suddenly Stevie was pure small boy again as he smiled adoringly up at his father, forcing Liza to think that perhaps she'd imagined his sombre thoughts.

'OK, Stevie, you can take William out to play now if you want to,' he said, grinning widely at the little boy's whoop as he and the dog made their rapid departure into the garden.

When he spoke again it was more to himself than to her. 'I have to go to Paris in the morning. It's a real nuisance but it can't be helped. I was hoping to make a start on the manuscripts but I'm afraid they'll have to wait a little longer.'

Liza gave a slight nod of her head to let him know she understood. 'Is there anything I could be getting on with on my own?'

His lips pursed as he considered. 'No, I'd rather we worked on it together.'

'As you wish.'

Anton turned abruptly back into the room and, almost as though inspiration had struck him, he asked, 'How's your French?'

Surprised, Liza answered, 'School-book, why?'

'Would you like to come?'

'Where? To Paris?'

'Yes. It'll only be for a few hours,

I'm afraid, but you're welcome to come if you like.'

Liza was surprised and delighted by the invitation and it showed. 'Sounds wonderful. I'd love to come.'

'We'll have to have to leave at the crack of dawn, I have a meeting at nine. That will mean you'll be left to your own devices for a couple of hours — would that bother you?'

'Of course not,' she laughed. 'I'm sure I can struggle through a couple of hours in Paris — on my own, or otherwise.'

Anton smiled. 'That's settled then,' he commented lightly, moving back to the window to resume his observation of his little son. Liza sat quietly waiting for him to speak again. She felt uncomfortable. She wasn't sure whether the interview was over or not and was just about to make a move when he turned to her, his dark eyes holding her strangely and saying quietly, 'A couple of friends are coming round tomorrow evening for a drink.

51

Would you care to join us?'

'I'd love to,' she murmured. 'I'd like to meet your friends.'

He smiled coldly. 'It's their wish, not mine. Personally, I'd rather you didn't.'

What a strange thing to say, thought Liza resentfully. Was he keeping her in her place as a hired assistant? Didn't he think she was good enough to meet his friends?

A little put out she retorted sharply, 'Then I won't!'

His brows lifted in sardonic surprise. 'I'm afraid I put that rather clumsily. My *friends* are a little . . . er . . . *different* . . . that's all I meant to say. I hardly think they'll be your kind of company.'

'Do you want me to meet them, or not?' she demanded.

'Not really, but it's nothing personal against you, I assure you. Still, I suppose it could be interesting.' He smiled that cold little smile again, conflicting expressions flickering in and out of his eyes, as though he was trying to make up his mind about something. Finally he said, this time with more warmth, 'Yes, Liza, perhaps I would like you to meet them after all. It might do them a world of good.'

At the crack of dawn next morning they set off for a nearby private airfield and boarded a Cessna. In no time at all, less than an hour in the air, Liza found herself cleared through the French passport control and in a taxi, driving briskly into the heart of that most romantic of cities, Paris.

Along the wide boulevards the chestnut trees were in full leaf and, at the end of the Champs Elysee, the Eiffel tower shimmered in the early morning sun. At her suggestion, Anton dropped her off at the Louvre and, arranging to meet her there in a couple of hours, he went off to his meeting.

She went inside the gallery. There would never be enough time to see everything so, like any tourist, Liza opted for the Mona Lisa and the

Venus di Milo, taking anything else as a bonus. Venus stopped her in her tracks. The feeling it gave her took her breath away. The serenity of the face and the texture of the marble gave her such a profound feeling that it was almost spiritual.

★ ★ ★

Anton was already waiting for her when she came out a couple of hours later. He called a taxi and treated her to a whirlwind tour of Montmartre until, paying off the cab, they found a table for two in the little square of Place du Tetre for lunch.

'Enjoying yourself?' he asked when they had eaten and the waiter had brought them their coffee.

'Oh, yes, who wouldn't? It really is the most beautiful of cities.'

Anton smiled. 'I suppose it is, and I'm glad you came, but you haven't seen a fraction of it. You've spent what little time you had in the Louvre. What caught your interest in there?'

'All of it, naturally,' Liza told him breathlessly, going on to tell him about the Venus. 'She gave me the most, oh, I don't know, the most profound feeling . . . ' Liza broke off, smiling and a little embarrassed as she saw his grin, enjoying her obvious delight and excitement.

'Don't stop there,' he prodded. 'I'm intrigued.' Then as Liza shook her head and took a sip of coffee, he went on in a more serious tone. 'Venus . . . the face of woman. I've never cared for her much.'

Liza gave him a long look. 'Don't you like women?'

He shrugged. 'That depends on the woman.'

'Oh?'

Anton smiled teasingly. 'Take you for instance.' Liza's eyes met his warily as she waited for him to go on. 'I could soon get to like a woman like you.'

'I'm flattered.'

He smiled again, challenging her

softly. 'You can't deny there's an attraction between us.'

To quell the emotions his gentle teasing was causing, Liza opted to take a sip of her coffee. No, she admitted to herself, she couldn't deny it. There was a very strong attraction. But she wasn't going to admit that to him.

'Paris makes you want to fall in love, doesn't it?' Anton went on softly.

'It would be hard not to, but let's not go into that.'

'Very sensible. After all, there's a lot of enjoyment this side of love, isn't there?' When Liza didn't answer he repeated, 'Isn't there?'

'Who could deny it?'

'But Paris apart, do you agree? When two people are attracted — I'm not asking lightly, Liza.'

'I know you're not.'

She fell silent for a few minutes, aware that he was forcing her into a decision; a decision that was vitally important as far as she was concerned. Should she encourage a relationship

56

that was beginning to mean far more to her than to him? Or should she withdraw before it all became far too involved? He was being more than fair but she wished he wasn't asking her for all that. She looked across to find that teasing, affectionate expression she was beginning to know so well.

'Living under the same roof,' she said quietly at last, 'and working closely together day after day may cause one or other of us to be tempted by our natural impulses, but any rashness may also cause some regret sooner or later. I think we'd both be making a terrible mistake.'

'Spoken bravely — and I'm glad.' He lifted his cup and took a sip, regarding her closely over the rim, then putting it down and asking, 'Do you think marriage is good for a man? Would it be hard for him to stay with one woman?'

Lisa sat back in her chair, her eyes guarded and curious. 'You were married once, Anton.'

'That was a long time ago,' he mused thoughfully. 'We were both too young, and it was too brief a time to put it to the test. Sometimes I find it hard to remember at all . . . Does that sound unfeeling?'

Liza shook her head slowly. 'No, not unfeeling. Nature has a way of healing. But I suppose if life has taught me anything at all, it is that you can't generalise about anything. Marriage, above all else, is what two individuals make of it. Fundamentally, I think it's natural for most women to want marriage — they see fulfilment in it. Men, on the other hand, fight shy of it. They seem to think it puts shackles on their freedom.'

Anton held her gaze, a deep sadness shadowing his eyes. 'But does it? Surely, marriage is an enlarging experience, isn't it? Not a prison. And I think that applies to both sexes.'

Liza took a long breath and said, half-smiling. 'Well, let me be rash enough to give you one conclusion I've come to. Remember the sonnet, '*Let me not to the marriage of true minds admit impediments . . .* '? Now, love of that kind between a man and a woman — and I think it's rare — adds another dimension to life instead of stifling it. And, one day, I hope to find such a love for myself.'

Anton didn't reply. Instead, he looked at her for a long time, aware as much Liza of the emotional awareness that was pulling them together. Then slowly he reached across and took hold of her hand, stroking his thumb along the tips of her fingers and saying softly, 'Liza Bancroft, what a surprising lady you are. How wonderful it would be if we could stay here together tonight, to perhaps discover such a love together.'

Slowly, she withdrew her trembling hands, draining her coffee quickly and forcing her clouded thoughts back to reality. 'I think it's time to go. Didn't I hear you tell the pilot we'd be back for four o'clock?'

Anton sat back, reaching for his

briefcase under the chair. 'You're right, of course. And it's almost a quarter to now.'

She heard his sigh as he stood up and took hold of her arm, steering her towards the taxi that would take them back to the airport and back to Lovell House.

4

Liza opted out of dinner on their return to Lovell House, pleading a slight headache. Besides, after three weeks apart, it would give Anton and Stevie some time to themselves; more to the point, she needed a few precious moments to herself.

Sitting on the bed, her arms hunched around her raised knees, she mulled over Anton's words, '*to discover such a love together*'. Oh heavens, she thought wearily, how could she face him again and not give herself away? More and more, he was taking over her senses.

But was it the same for him? Somehow Liza didn't think so. He wanted an affair — he'd even offered her one — but that was as far as he was prepared to go. It wasn't going to be easy now to smother her feelings for Anton Demegar, but she knew she must.

Why, oh, why, did she have to feel this way? It was bad enough having to cope with the anguish of her own emotions now that she'd let him know that such a situation was impossible, and even worse, knowing that Anton's desires for her were nowhere near as deep.

Liza smiled wrily, coming back to earth as she heard the soft tap on the door. The headache which had originally been fiction was fast becoming fact.

'How do you feel now?' Milly asked, settling down a tray on the small table by Liza's bed.

'Much better, thanks.'

'Get some of this soup down you, it'll do you more good than any of that stuff you ate in Paris.'

Liza smiled and did as she was told, listening to Milly's dialogue on the dangers of eating anything 'foreign' and that 'there was nothing like good homemade food to put a lining on your stomach.'

'Would you prefer to stay in your room tonight?' she continued. 'I could always tell Mr Anton you don't feel up to meeting his friends.'

'No, Milly, I'm fine,' Liza reiterated firmly. 'And I'd quite like to meet them. Who are they, do you know?'

Milly gave a short sniff. 'I know them all right. Two of them are quite nice — Mr Hugo, for instance. He works for Mr Anton, a pilot I think, and they've been friends since they were at school together. Then there's Miss Deans — Marjorie. She's a quiet lass, never much to say but always nice and polite, a real lady, if you know what I mean. Mr Hugo and Miss Deans are engaged to be married. But the other one — the *American*!'

Liza hid a smile but didn't interrupt, Milly was in full flow now and gossiping on, 'She's Miss Gerhardt — *Charity* Gerhardt, if you please.' The woman's eyebrows arched as her tone expressed even more disapproval, 'And you know what they say about Charity, don't you?'

'No, Milly, what?'

'It's a cold thing, and they don't come much colder than that one.'

'I take it you don't care for her very much.'

Milly sniffed again and picked up Liza's tray. 'That's not for me to say, is it? But I don't think she's good for Mr Anton.'

Liza glanced up quickly. Suddenly Milly's words were desperately loaded. 'Good for him? Why?' she parried lightly, 'Is she a special friend of his?'

'I think she'd like to be,' Milly replied hotly, then lowering her wheezy voice again in a conspiritorial whisper she added, 'she's Miss Elizabeth's friend really, but that Gerhardt woman's never off the phone when he's home.' Straightening her little round body the housekeeper took a step towards the door. 'Anyway, I've gossiped enough. If you're coming down you'd better start getting changed, it's nearly half past seven.'

Milly's mention of Anton's sister sparked off Liza's curiosity again. Why did the girl intrigue her so? Why did she sense such secrecy whenever anyone spoke of her? Swinging her legs off the bed she asked quietly, 'Milly, what's Elizabeth like?'

Milly put the tray down again, folding her short arms across the wide expanse of her bosom. A look of worry shadowed her sharp, bird-like eyes as she pursed her lips and regarded Liza. 'She's not been well, not well at all.'

'What's the matter?'

'Doctor Magill gave it a long fancy name but, if you ask me, it's all nerves. She's very high-strung, you know, always has been — just like her mother. Mr Anton thinks the world of her and, sometimes, she plays on it, runs rings round him. He spoils her if you ask me. Last year, when she took ill, she went into a nursing home, a big fancy place near York, and she seemed a lot better when she came home.'

'Anyway, for reasons best known to himself, Mr Anton packed her off to Bermuda to convalesce — not Scarborough or Whitley Bay, where she would have been better off if you ask me.' Milly gave a deep sigh, picking up the tray again, 'But there, nobody ever does ask me and it's none of my business . . . ' adding quietly, ' . . . nor yours either.'

Liza took special care when she dressed to go downstairs. Looking at herself in the Cheval mirror she knew she looked good, but when she reached the top of the stairs she found herself moving like a mechanical doll. Her lips felt stiff as she pinned on a smile and a cold clamminess clung to her body.

Anton's guests had arrived, she could hear the sound of their subdued laughter and the clinking of glasses coming from the patio as she reached the bottom stair. Anton was waiting for her in the shadow of the hallway, striding forward and looking at her with a strange speculation as he took her hand, his touch crystallising all her fears. *She had fallen hopelessly in love with him*!

'Ready for the fray?' he murmured expressionlessly.

'Will it be that bad?'

'It may have its moments.'

He led her outside. The patio was lit with muted spotlights, revealing three people seated together at a wrought-iron table, one man and two women. The man sprang to his feet the moment they appeared and reached their side in a couple of strides.

'So this is your new assistant,' he said, his clear blue eyes appraising Liza as he lifted her hand to his lips.

'It is,' Anton agreed blandly. 'May I introduce Ms Liza Bancroft, and this, Liza, is Hugo Stout. A word in your ear, though, he should come with a Government Health warning — he imagines he's God's gift and treats women accordingly.'

'Don't believe him, Liza. I'm as

innocent as the day is long.'

'That'll be the day,' Anton responded in a hard voice, leading her towards the two women.

The dark-haired girl was about twenty-five, plump, jolly-looking and smiling at Liza with dark eyes. Her dress was simple but expensive, and on her engagement finger Liza spotted an enormous solitaire diamond.

They shook hands but Liza found her attention wandering towards the other girl. This woman was stunningly beautiful. She sat elegantly casual in a white silk suit that would have set Liza back at least a year's salary. The girl's fine, silver-blonde hair was cut to reach the collar of her expensive suit, cascading from a centre parting to fall loosely back behind her small, petal-shaped ears.

'Liza, this is Charity,' she heard Anton say. 'Charity Gerhardt.'

Liza met the cool gaze as they touched hands. Charity's beautiful eyes were narrowed with a look of speculation as she sized Liza up in the few brief seconds of their introduction.

'Darling,' Charity purred. 'You didn't tell us she was so pretty.'

Liza laughed nervously, a little uncomfortable by the girl's cat-like scrutiny and she silently blessed Hugo's interruption as he handed her a glass of wine, giving her the excuse to turn away.

The evening wore on pleasantly. The talk drifted from one thing to another, interspersed by laughter and much banter between Anton and Hugo. It was sometime later when Charity turned to Anton and asked, 'Did you see anything of Mike when you were in Paris today?'

Liza couldn't be sure, but somehow she sensed a slight edge in the atmosphere as she heard Anton's reply.

'I haven't seen Mike in months — you know that, Charity.'

Charity Gerhardt gave a shrug of her elegant shoulders. 'I thought you may have run into him.'

'Well, I didn't. And you know Mike as well as I. You never know where he is half the time.'

'That's true enough . . . '

Liza looked at Anton as he reached for another bottle of wine. Taut lines had suddenly hardened his mouth, setting off alarm bells somewhere in the back of her mind. Mike! That name again! Something was wrong!

Liza gave herself a mental shake. Why should there be tension just because Charity mentioned this mysterious Mike? And what possible connection could this little gathering have with the couple in church yesterday? After all, there were millions of Mikes in the world. Her own brother had Michael as his middle name!

Shrugging off her misgivings she turned back to the conversation, responding to Marjorie's question about her work. 'Yes, Marjorie, I'm fascinated by the Plantagenets.'

Hugo's fiancée laughed teasingly towards Anton. 'As much as Anton?'

And at Liza's 'I suppose so,' she laughed again, 'I truly believe our friend here is in love with that Queen of Edward's. What was her name . . . Elizabeth?'

Anton cut in sharply, almost roughly, as he poured the wine. 'Elizabeth Woodville is the one you mean, Marj, and I'm not! She was a hardnosed troublemaker if ever there was one.'

'Some women are like that,' Hugo butted in. 'They twist us poor men around their little fingers.'

Amid the derisive laughter that followed Hugo's remark, Liza heard Charity's goading, 'I hope you don't think I'm one of those, Anton darling.'

The girl's words were like a douche of cold water and Liza stiffened in her chair as she saw her slide her arms around his neck, and Anton, responding, slipped his arm around her waist, pulling her against him before he kissed her.

Liza felt sick. She tried to concentrate on the wine but all she could see was

Anton's face, Anton's broad shoulders, Anton's arms around another girl.

'Darling,' Charity purred when Anton finally released her, 'don't you think it's time you told them our news?'

'You tell them, darling.'

Liza sat very still. For the briefest of seconds Anton turned to her with a look of deep intensity. His look disturbed her. But even so, when she heard Charity's 'Anton and I have decided to get married', she was conscious only of the sudden icy chill in the night air. Her face felt drained of colour; she wanted to leap out of her chair and rush away from these people — to get into her car and drive away from them as far and as fast as she could.

But of course she didn't. Some inherent and stubborn streak would not let her. If she had been fool enough to fall in love with a man who loved someone else, then she ought to have the integrity — not to mention the guts — to stay and finish the work she'd set out to do.

The celebrations continued until, just after eleven, Hugo and Marjorie took their leave, giving Liza the opportunity to excuse herself as well. Moving like a robot, she said her 'goodnights' and walked towards the door when Anton observed quietly,

'We'll make a start on the manuscript in the morning, Liza. Will nine o'clock be OK?'

Standing there, half in half out of the patio doorway, Liza turned back, aware of two bright spots of colour burning in her cheeks. 'Nine o'clock will be fine.'

Liza didn't go to bed immediately. Instead she cleaned off her make-up and switched on the television, catching the closing scenes of an old black and white Bette Davis weepie. When it ended she switched off the light but, instead of getting into bed, she walked over to the window, opening it and looking out.

A low slung American car was still standing in the drive and, after a

73

few minutes, Anton and Charity came strolling arm in arm out of the house towards it. Their voices were low and muffled and, as Anton opened the driver's door, Charity slid her arms around his neck.

Liza moved away from the window and climbed into bed. She had no desire to witness their embraces tonight and she closed her eyes, willing sleep. She could hear Charity's voice quite clearly now and Liza turned over, pulling the sheets up around her head. It made no difference. The woman's words, more vibrant now, came clearly in the still night air.

'*Why wasn't it marked?*'

Anton's reply came back disconnected, incomprehensible, then Charity's voice again, louder, '*She asks for it!*'

Now Anton's voice again, this time clear and cold. '*If anything should happen to her . . . !*'

Liza heard the sound of footsteps moving around on the gravel, then the sound of a car door opening and closing, and Anton's voice again, angry and harsh, *'That's blackmail! And the date's already been set for Hazlehurst!'*

The car started up and, over its hum came Charity's clipped response, *'And do something about that wretched dog — keep it away from . . . '*

The rest of her words were lost in the rev of an engine and a moment later Liza heard the car speed away down the drive. She lay still for a long time after that. Hazlehurst! Wasn't that the place Anton had warned her against?

Liza forced herself to think reasonably. She told herself bitterly that she mustn't read anything into what she had overheard. She was being absurd to feel alarmed by what was probably nothing more than a lover's tiff.

But her thoughts drifted back again. What kind of lovers would quarrel about blackmail? Liza remembered how tense Anton had been earlier and how those alarm bells had sounded at their talk of Mike. What was going on here? She knew something was! Something was wrong — very wrong.

At last Liza slipped into a troubled sleep, her mind disturbed by flickers of dreams which made no sense, and which her memory failed to retain. They all contained Anton, however — she couldn't escape him even in her dreams. The last thing she heard was the patter of rain against the window, signalling an end to the long hot spell.

5

Liza's head swam back to wakefulness. She turned a pair of sleepy eyes to the window, yawned, and rolled onto her back. Then, reaching for her clock, she let out a small cry of alarm to see that it was already a quarter to nine. In the space of fifteen minutes she had showered, dressed and was gulping down hot coffee in Milly's kitchen.

Stevie was on the point of departure for school, his small face barely visible beneath the yellow sou'wester. ' 'Bye, Liza. 'Bye, William,' his piping little voice called excitedly, scooping up his schoolbag. 'Norman's taking me to the bus on the tractor.'

Milly waved them off. Her wispy hair was still in curlers and she reminded Liza of a latter-day Medusa, but, closing the door behind them, she turned sternly to Liza, 'Mr Anton's been in his study since half past eight,' she said, a hint of reprimand in her voice. 'He's a stickler for time — I'd get a move on if I were you.'

'I hardly slept last night, Milly,' Liza explained. 'It's not like me at all.' She gulped down the last of her coffee and made her way to Anton's study.

It was just going on nine fifteen. Anton didn't look round, but there was no mistaking the significant glance he gave to his watch.

'Sorry to be late on my first morning,' she apologised. 'I overslept, I'm afraid. It must have been the wine. I'm not used to it. I'll see that it doesn't happen again.'

'No matter.' Anton turned, sifting through a sheaf of papers. 'We'll start with the beheading of Lord Hastings.'

She was ravenously hungry by the time Milly brought in a tray of tea and biscuits. When the housekeeper had gone, leaving Liza to pour, she watched Anton's movements as he took his cup and went to stand by the window. He seemed distracted. His brows were drawn sharply into a frown as he stared out over the wild, rain-drenched landscape, and the thing that struck Liza most were the lines of deep unhappiness etched across his face.

He lifted the cup to his lips, taking a sip. And, as he stood there so tensely, Liza was reminded of Stevie's face yesterday. It held that same strained look of sadness and she wondered again what could be putting it there. Was it to do with his sister? Or was it to do with the argument with Charity last night? She longed to ask but didn't dare.

Liza took another biscuit, concern for this man and his little son evident in her eyes. After a moment she asked quietly, 'Are you all right, Anton? You look worried.'

He turned sharply, throwing her a

guarded look. 'Worried? Why should I be worried?'

'I don't know, but I have the feeling that something's bothering you.'

His eyes were still withdrawn. He glanced at her, then glanced away. 'You're imagining things.'

Liza hoped she was, and was vaguely aware of her relief, but so strong was her intuition that it made little impression on her. She gave a small shrug and said nothing, stealing another glance at his profile as he came back to his desk.

'Shall we get on?' he said, flicking open the manuscript again.

'Yes, of course.'

They worked on for another hour, moving from William Hastings' untimely end to the eve of Bosworth Field.

'Richard was lucky to have Sir Francis Lovell as a friend, don't you think?' Liza asked, observing Anton's dark eyes. 'Does this house — Lovell House — have any connection?'

Anton laughed, and Liza was relieved to find his good humour returning. 'I'm afraid not. The Lovells who built this place were yeomen. They were well-to-do, I'll admit, but not the landed gentry of medieval England. The Lovell line ran out several generations ago and my great-great-great grandmother married a Frenchman, one Jean-Thierry Demegar. We've been here ever since.'

Liza gave a little disappointed sigh. 'That's a pity.'

Anton came and perched himself on the edge of her desk, taking the remaining biscuit, biting into it and eyeing her with amused speculation. 'What's a pity?' he asked. 'The fact that we're not related to Sir Francis, or because my great-great-great grandmother married a Frenchman?'

'I meant the fact that you're not related. I've always had a soft spot for the Lovells.'

'Why? Because of his loyalty?'

'Yes, probably. He stuck to Richard through thick and thin, it's a quality that's rare these days.'

'That depends . . . and I'm sorry to

81

disappoint you about Sir Francis.' He smiled at her softly. 'But we yeomen Lovells are every bit as loyal to our friends, too.' Liza saw the shadow come back into his eyes, sensed a siight tightening of the mouth as he added bitterly, ' . . . we value trust, and sometimes we pay a heavy price for it.' He looked at her warily. 'Now, back to Jane Shore.'

They worked on, losing themselves in the subject that was so fascinating to both of them. At one o'clock they took a break for lunch and by the time Stevie came home a little after four, they'd covered much more than either realised.

Anton went out to meet him and Liza smiled to herself as she heard them fooling about at the back of the house. Carrying on with her work, she looked up as the phone rang on Anton's desk. It rang several times before she realised that no-one was going to answer it so, getting up, she picked up the receiver herself.

'Anton?' A man's voice came down the line.

'No, he isn't here, but if you'll hold on, I'll get him for you . . . '

'Is that you, Liza? It's me — Hugo Stout!'

Liza thought she'd recognised the voice and answered, 'Hello, Hugo. Anton's out in the kitchen with Stevie, I'll get him for you . . . '

'No . . . just a minute, Liza, there's something I want to ask you.'

'Yes? What is it?'

'I'm curious. Have you any connection with Mike Ban — '

There was a click. Someone had picked up the extension in the hall. Anton's voice broke into Hugo's question, interrupting sharply, 'Hugo? Anton here. Anything wrong?' Then to Liza he added, 'It's OK, Liza. I'll take it now.'

He waited until she'd put down the receiver. Liza was puzzled. She knew Hugo Stout was about to ask if she was connected with Mike Bancroft in any way and what was the harm in that? Why had Anton so rudely and deliberately cut them off like that?

But, when Anton came back into the office, she caught her breath. If ever there was a look of murder in anyone's eyes, it was in Anton's at that moment.

She waited a while, watching for his tension to ebb, and when it did she summoned up all her resolve, saying with as much coolness as she could muster, 'Hugo was just about to ask me about my connection with a Mike Bancroft. Do you know why he should?'

She didn't miss the startled jerk of his head as he looked up sharply to face her. 'Why should I?'

'As Hugo's friend, I wondered if you knew this Mike Bancroft, too.'

The strained silence that fell between them was broken only by the steady beat of rain against the window. Anton's strange challenging expression puzzled her. It was a look of urgency, of extraordinary reaction. Then he spoke.

His tone was calm, cold, 'Bancroft isn't such an uncommon name — nor is Mike.'

'But I *do* know someone called Mike Bancroft — my brother.'

Anton stood up, moving to the filing cabinet and opening it. 'I thought your brother's name was Charlie.'

'So it is. But he has a middle name, too, and that is Michael.'

There was the briefest of pauses before he made a cautious response, 'Mere coincidence.'

'Is it, Anton? How do I know that? Do you know this Mike Bancroft?'

'Why on earth should I?'

'That's just the point! Why should you? What's going on, Anton? The man I heard in the church spoke of a Mike, is it the same one? Is it my brother everyone's talking about?'

Anton didn't answer so Liza stood up, too, and went to stand by his side. She wanted to see into his eyes; to see if he was hiding something from her. She needed to satisfy herself that she was mistaken — that she was making a mountain out of a molehill, and that it was, as Anton suggested, mere coincidence. She needed to be convinced that her brother had nothing to do with any of this, and that he certainly wasn't the same Mike who had frightened the girl in the church so much.

Anton's hands had tightened around the drawer handle. His knuckles were showing white against his skin and she was suddenly very afraid.

Slowly, he turned, his face white and serious. He took hold of her hand and held it in both of his, an unexpected response that made her look at him inquiringly. It was just a touch of hands, nothing more, but all at once her heart was beating wildly, beating with a strange mixture of fear and wonder.

'Do you have any idea of what it means to me to have you here?' he asked softly.

Liza lifted her eyes, looking at him

and shaking her head.

Slowly, almost reluctantly, he pulled her close. For long, stunned minutes neither spoke as Anton held her against his chest. His touch was tender and she could feel his breath against her hair, warm and moving. Irrationally, she felt suddenly unbelievably happy. It was one of those rare moments that makes sense without making any sense at all. He held her for only a moment, but it could have been that he'd been holding her for ever.

'Liza . . . '

His voice came so soft that she only just heard him. His kiss, when it came, was exquisite, releasing all the parched feelings she'd locked away inside. He felt her response and kissed her again and again, 'Liza . . . Liza . . . Liza . . . '

But suddenly, like a cold ugly shadow, the memory of his engagement crawled into her mind. With great determination she pulled herself away. 'Stop, Anton . . . For heaven's sake, stop . . . ' Liza didn't want to stop. She fought hard against her innate sense of right and wrong, that old practical streak which she tried so hard to suppress. 'Please, Anton . . . This is crazy!'

Anton's eyes were glazed as his hands fell away. 'So what if it *is crazy*? What does it matter?'

Liza put up a hand to silence him, 'It matters a lot. Haven't we forgotten something?'

He looked suddenly bleak and didn't answer her. Drawing himself up, he ran a hand through his thick dark curls, his expression desperate.

'I should have known you would have principles.' His face was almost grey in the watery light, etched with bitterness and the weary cynicism she had come to know so well. 'It's difficult . . . Sometimes, things are not what they seem.' He looked bitterly unhappy at that moment. He sighed and said very quietly, 'I know this sounds crazy, but don't believe everything you see.

It's a funny old world.'

Liza moved back to lean against her desk, supporting herself with the heels of her hands. She had her back to Anton and turned her head towards the window, looking at the rain. 'I believe what I saw last night, Anton — you and Charity together. And I remember you saying you were going to marry her.' The rain was running down the pane in tiny rivulets, reminding her of little teardrops. She heard Anton's long sigh and she felt him come to stand behind her. His arms came around her waist and she felt his face against the back of her head, his lips touch the black silk of her hair. Then his lips moved to brush against her neck.

'Trust me, Liza,' he murmured. 'That's all I have a right to ask. I didn't mean for this to happen, but,' his voice lowered to a whisper, 'please, please, trust me.'

His words, soft in her ear and sounding so full of unhappiness, confused her. She knew he was filled with an intense awareness of a new, strange, crazy mixed-up emotion, and she knew without doubt that she truly wanted to trust him.

Liza swallowed hard, willing her heart to calm its stifling beating. Slowly, Anton pulled her round to face him and, when he spoke again, his words were filled with such intensity that she felt herself grow faint.

'All I'm asking is that you trust me.' He reached up a hand and smoothed a strand of hair away from her cheek, 'and to be careful — *very* careful. I can't explain yet, perhaps I never can, but this I promise you. Some things are not what they seem, and no-one, *no-one*,' he repeated, ' . . . is who they appear to be.'

Thoroughly confused, Liza gave a small shake of her head and lifted dark questioning eyes to his. 'What are you saying, Anton? What are you trying to tell me? That Charity is not who she seems to be — the girl you intend to marry?'

At her words anger gripped Liza's heart. His words had been said with such finality that she almost hoped she'd imagined them.

'Then what was all that about?' she demanded coldly. 'Do you make a habit of making passes at every likely female who happens to work for you? Is it all part of the job?' Liza knew her words sounded petty and childish but, nevertheless, she went on, 'This may surprise you, Anton, but I want you to know it — and know it fast! I'm not, nor ever have been, casual in my affections!'

'I never thought you were.'

They stood silently, locked in each other's gaze, but when Anton didn't offer any more explanation, Liza turned away. She walked around her desk and sat down, 'Do you wish to do any more work today?' she asked, her tone both cold and dismissive.

She didn't look up as his reply came back, 'No, you can put the manuscripts away. It's unlikely that either of us could concentrate now.'

As he walked to the door she glanced up, but without turning back he walked through. She couldn't be sure, he spoke so quietly, but as he went out she heard his words, 'Trust is something I'd hoped I'd find . . .'

He let the sentence hang, closing the door softly behind him.

6

The next few weeks passed without incident. Liza and Anton worked well as a team, making rapid strides on the manuscript; Liza cool and efficient, Anton sometimes a little erratic but possessed of the talent and flair that made him such an outstanding historical writer. Their main topic of conversation centred around their work and not once did he give any sign that he wanted to hold her again.

Quite the reverse was true in fact. It was almost as though he wanted to put as much space between them as possible. If they touched accidentally he would withdraw quickly, as though any physical contact with her would burn.

Today she was alone in the study. Earlier, she had seen Anton drive off somewhere and she was sitting, head bent, over a map of medieval

Tewkesbury, measuring the distance between the battleground and the Severn river, and working out how long it would have taken the Lancastrians to reach the safety of the Welsh bank if their dash for freedom had come off.

A light tap-tap brought her back to the present and, looking up, the blonde head of Stevie appeared around the door.

'Dad's left a message for you and I nearly forgot.'

'Oh?'

'He asked me to ask you to have dinner with us tonight.'

Liza smiled and shook her head. Why couldn't he have asked her himself? Yet, to have dinner with Anton and Stevie would have been wonderful, but knowing it was likely that Charity would be Anton's guest, too, was more than she could bear. 'Tell your Dad thanks, Stevie, but if he doesn't mind, I'll eat with Milly and Norman in the kitchen as usual.'

'And William,' the little boy reminded her.

'Of course . . . ' Liza smiled again. 'And William.'

Stevie turned to go, then he paused, looking back, 'Dad says he'll teach me to fly when I'm old enough.'

'Do you want to be a pilot, too?'

He gave a disgusted sigh and thrust his hands deep into the pockets of his jeans. 'Yes, but I'll have to wait a long time for that. I'm fed-up with not being old enough for anything, it isn't fair!'

Liza inclined her head sympathetically, 'Life does seem unfair sometimes, I agree.' She smiled mirthlessly. How true that was! Life could be horribly unfair! It was unfair that she loved this boy's father so much when he had already made his choice of wife. She looked across at Anton's little son as he waited in the doorway. 'Never mind, Stevie,' she said brightly. 'You'll soon be flying all over the place, you'll see.'

Stevie nodded vigorously. 'I'spect by

that time pilots will all be astronauts.'

'I suppose they will. Just think, you could be another Captain Kirk and fly a ship like the Enterprise.'

Stevie's eyes gleamed with open admiration for Liza, bright in their respect that she should equate him with his hero. 'Are you a 'Trekkie', too?'

'I most certainly am.'

Stevie beamed again and turned to go. 'Just wait 'til I tell Dad you're a 'Trekkie'!'

The door closed softly behind him and Liza went back to her work. Much later, looking out of the window at the grey overcast sky, Anton's car pulled up into the drive diverting her attention. She tried not to care as she watched him dash across the drive and into the house, his arm supporting the beautiful girl at his side. Liza sighed, quelling the surge of jealousy that ran through her. Her feelings for him were becoming quite a problem.

Forcing her attention back to her work she tried to tell herself it was all a waste of time and energy, and that it was her bad luck that she should fall for this strange, enigmatic man when he made it so plain he loved someone else!

By six o'clock Liza's fingers were aching. Since Anton's arrival back at the house she'd thrown herself into her work, completing all the alterations and corrections he had marked, and a glance at her watch told her she had worked far longer than she'd intended.

She made her way along the passage towards the kitchen, but her steps slowed as she found Anton waiting for her by the sitting-room door. His eyes, cold and impersonal, swept over her slender figure in its dark blue skirt and pretty spotted blouse.

'What a pity we are to be deprived of your company this evening,' he commented smoothly.

Liza smiled politely and answered firmly, 'I'm sure you'll manage.'

Anton's eyes through the heavy dark lashes showed a brief flicker of amusement as he stood barring her way. 'There must be some way I can make you change your mind . . . '

Liza gave a slight shrug of her shoulders but, before she could answer, the sitting-room door opened as Charity came out. 'Anton, how long are you going to be?'

Anton's eyes narrowed as he turned to his fiancee, 'I won't be a moment, Charity — I have to discuss something with Liza.'

Charity fixed Liza with an icy gaze. 'Won't it wait?'

'No, it won't. I'll be with you in a moment.'

Charity held them in her gaze for a few more seconds before, with a fluid motion of her graceful body, she turned and went back into the room. Anton turned back to Liza quickly and this time, when he spoke, there was a note of urgency in his tone. 'Liza, I insist that you join me for dinner.'

Liza looked up into his face, her heart lurching at the look of tenderness in the depths of his eyes. With a deep sigh she replied, 'It's impossible, Anton.'

He gave a small grin, 'You'll be quite safe. I'm not a cheat, Liza, if that's what you're thinking. I would like your company, that's all . . . ' There was a moment's pause while Liza tried to decide what to do, then he added more softly, 'I *need* your company tonight.'

Liza searched his face looking for a grain of insincerity but could see none. 'Wouldn't Charity disapprove?' she asked finally.

'Charity has nothing to do with it-- anyway, she won't be here. She's going back into town shortly. But how can I convince you that you'll be perfectly safe? I promise you — you have my word on it.' He smiled suddenly. It was a smile at once tender and yet holding such gentle pleading that Liza found herself smiling, too.

With a sigh of resignation she murmured, 'Do I have a choice? Or is having dinner with my boss a part of my duty?'

'It is if that's the only way I can persuade you.'

'In that case,' she relented, 'there isn't much choice, is there?'

At last Anton moved to let her pass, 'It's a good choice,' then adding very softly, *Loyaultie me lie!*'

Liza lifted startled eyes to look into his face again, but he had turned quickly to go back into the sitting-room. Slowly, she made her way to the kitchen, her heart beating faster as she recognised the motto of Richard Plantagent — *'Loyaultie me lie.'* Loyalty binds me! What was he trying to tell her? And to whom was he vowing his loyalty? Why, oh why, did he always have to speak in riddles?

★ ★ ★

It was much later in the evening and Liza was curled up on the rug by the dining-room fire. 'You didn't put quite enough on.'

Anton threw her a puzzled look. 'Quite enough what?'

'Salt and vinegar.'

He grinned, 'I'm sorry, I'll remember next time. Want some beer?'

'No thanks. It makes all the difference, you know.'

'What does?'

'Putting the salt and vinegar on before you bring them home — it soaks in and improves the taste.'

Anton chuckled, a sound that conceded she was absolutely right. 'I believe you, thousands wouldn't,' he said, his amused glance following Liza's movements as she reached up to switch off the television.

It had been a wonderful evening, Anton and Stevie falling in completely with her idea of a fish and chip supper by the fire. Anton had driven into Daneshaw to get them, and when he'd got back, they'd eaten them, Japanese style, at a small table in front of the fire. A short while ago Anton had carried a happy little boy off to bed and was now sitting with Liza on the rug.

He moved to sit beside her, swivelling himself around until his arm rested lightly on her shoulder. It felt wonderful to be as near to him as this and Liza summoned all her willpower to stop herself from reaching up and run her fingers through his curly mass of hair. 'I can't remember when I've enjoyed an evening so much,' he murmured contentedly. 'Lovell House feels like home for the first time in years.' He smiled at her, his face just inches away from her own. 'You seem to have the knack of helping me relax.'

His smile was so tender that it made Liza catch her breath, conscious of a small aching feeling deep down inside her. She smiled back and shook her head, not trusting herself to speak.

They sat together in the firelight, leaning back against the heavy armchair and enjoying the comfortable silence that surrounded them. Anton hadn't said a word about Charity all evening and Liza had been glad of it. Whenever she thought of his beautiful fiancée which was almost all the time — she felt an uncomfortable emotion in the pit of her stomach. When she finally recognised what it was, she hadn't realised before how deeply it could affect her. It was the vilest feeling of all — jealousy!

Liza kept telling herself that it was all so ridiculous. After all, she hardly knew Anton. She hadn't even known of his existence until a few short weeks ago, but now she was behaving like a silly, moonstruck child.

Anton stirred, taking his hand from her shoulder and propping his head against his hand.

Liza edged herself up a little against the chair and retreated once more into her safe protected self. She must stay in control of her mind — if not her heart.

Anton felt her move and asked, 'Comfortable?'

Liza nodded. 'I'm fine, but I think it's time for bed.'

Anton's soft laugh came against her cheek. 'Funny, I was just thinking the same thing.'

Liza turned to him quickly, seeing in his eyes the look she knew was mirrored in her own. 'I meant that it is getting late, Anton,' she murmured.

He made a small face, stirred and stretched his arms above his head. 'I know what you meant but it seems a pity to let this evening end. Shall we have a nightcap?'

Liza laughed, trying desperately to break the emotionally-charged atmosphere that was drawing them together like a magnet. 'On top of fish and chips? No thanks, I'd never sleep,' She scrambled to her feet, holding out an arm to help him up, 'Come on, we've a lot of work to get through tomorrow.'

Anton took her hand, his dark eyes smiling but making no move to rise. 'Don't go yet, Liza . . . Not yet . . . '

'Please, Anton, we must. Let's not start something we can't finish.'

His voice became nothing more than a whisper. 'You want me as much as I want you, I can feel it.' But as Liza tugged her hand away he relented, standing up with a sigh, 'OK, I'm sorry, you win — I have no right . . . '

'No, Anton, you have no right.' Liz put her hand to silence him as he started to speak again. 'And you gave me your promise!'

Anton's hands fell away abruptly. 'Yes, I did, didn't I?' His face held an anguished look. 'I wish . . . I wish . . . '

Liza turned her dark anxious eyes to his, 'What do you wish, Anton?'

He gave her a small shrug, avoiding her gaze, 'Oh, nothing . . . ' He paused for a moment, then went on quickly. 'It isn't just that I long for you, and you know that's true,' he paused again briefly before adding quietly, 'You're becoming important to me, Liza, and I don't want to hurt you.'

'Why should you hurt me?'

His look became bitter, 'I don't want to pull you into my world as it is right now. I don't want you to be a part of something you don't understand, and where you could never be happy.'

Liza stiffened slightly. 'What is it I'm not able to understand? I'm not a complete moron — try me, and explain what it is that could make me so unhappy.'

She wanted his confidence. She would do anything for him now. She wanted to tell him how she felt about him, but she couldn't. She couldn't tell Anton that she loved him, and felt she had the right to make him love her back — Charity or no Charity. All was fair in love and war, wasn't it? And Charity wasn't his wife yet!

But something told her it wasn't that that was keeping him away from her, it was something more. Something was eating away at him; something he was keeping to himself; and whatever that something was, she made up her mind to find it out. 'Try me, Anton,' she urged again. 'You'll find I'm not the type to shrink from something once I know what I'm up against.'

'I know you aren't, but I'm not prepared to risk it.'

His evasiveness began to irritate her, making her snap angrily, 'Stop talking in riddles! Tell me what I have to be so careful about. And tell me what you meant when you said things aren't as they seem.'

'I can't — not yet.'

'Does Charity know what it is?'

He gave a short, bitter laugh. 'Oh yes, Charity knows all about it. Now, please, Liza, let it drop, I've said far too much as it is.'

Liza let out a small, surprised laugh. 'You haven't said a word I understand yet, Anton.'

'Believe me, it's better that you don't know. I made a mistake tonight. I've let my feelings run away with me. From now on we'll treat each other merely as colleagues and I want you to put all the things I've said tonight right out of your head.'

Liza gave an exasperated sigh. 'How can I, Anton? First I see your sister in the church and yet you deny it — '

'It wasn't my sister!'

Ignoring him Liza went on impatiently, 'Then I hear a weird conversation about Mike Bancroft — and Hugo thinks I may be connected with him! And, here you are, warning me to be careful; not to believe what I see; to close my eyes to whatever's going on around me. What's it all about? Are you trying to drive me mad?'

'Have you finished?'

Liza took a deep breath. 'No, not quite . . . ' Her dark eyes held his steadily. 'There's one more thing I'd like to ask.'

His face was a mask. 'Well, I can't guarantee an answer, but ask away if you must.'

'Do you *truly* love Charity?'

There, it was out! Suddenly, Liza felt very cold. That tiny germ of doubt had forced her to blurt it out and, too late, she wished she hadn't. He was silent for a long moment and Liza at least had the satisfaction of seeing his skin darken under his tan. Her throat tightened as the hardness came into his eyes and when, at last, he spoke his voice was empty of all emotion.

His words came out like chips of ice. 'What I feel for Charity is my affair. You shouldn't have asked me that!'

Liza felt terrible. Anton's bitter anger was blazingly apparent as he turned towards the door. She had the feeling that he was a part of a puzzle that was far too intricate for easy answers, yet she hated to be the cause of the hurt annoyance that was showing so clearly now on his face.

Liza felt herself move towards him, reaching out to touch his arm. 'I'm sorry, Anton, I had no right to ask you that. Please, forgive me.'

His hand rested on hers for the briefest of moments as he responded with a wintry smile, 'You're forgiven.'

109

He held her hand against his chest. His heart was beating as though he'd run a marathon and the irises of his dark eyes were the colour of claret. 'Liza, I'm not playing games. Don't be suspicious of me, and please don't look at me like that. It's because I care for you that I don't want you to get hurt.'

'Anton . . . ' Liza was bedazzled by the violence of her emotions and her brain was struggling vainly to make some logic of his words. 'You ask me to trust you and I do. It goes against all my instincts, but I do trust you. Why can't you trust me back? Why can't you tell me what's going on? Why do I have to be so careful?'

Anton gave a bleak smile. 'You're persistent, I'll give you that. And I'm probably exaggerating things out of all proportion, making it sound more than it is, but, until the trouble on the moor is cleared up, just do as I say and be careful.'

Liza's exasperation was simmering

towards boiling point now. 'Oh, come on, Anton! There's more to it than that, I know there is.'

'Just do as I ask,' he replied wearily. 'Now, go to bed and get some sleep, it's been a long day.'

Anton opened the door, then he went through without another word.

7

Anton had already left the house when Liza got up next morning. Listlessly, she toyed with a piece of toast, watching Milly clean imaginary specks of dirt from the patterned tile floor.

'Do you know where Stevie is?' she asked. 'I've promised to drive him to school this morning.'

'He was up before daylight. His dog got out yesterday so he's gone to the lower fields with Norman to look for him.'

Liza glanced quickly at the housekeeper's stooping figure. 'Does William roam often?'

'No, not that much, although he's been out all night once before.' She shook her head. 'Stevie gets so upset when he's not here.'

Liza nodded in agreement, looking morosely out of the window at the rain.

'They'll be soaked — I hope they find him soon.' She sighed. 'Pity about the weather, I would have liked to ride on the moor today.'

The housekeeper looked up quickly, her mouth tightening. 'Best you keep off that moor if you know what's good for you,' she muttered. 'There's no good comes of going up there — it's bedevilled.'

Liza laughed in astonishment. 'You're not another one who believes in witches are you, Milly?'

But the look on Milly's face was deadly serious as she went over to the sink to wring out the cleaning cloth. 'There's been a lot of strange things going on up there this summer. People have seen and heard things — especially at night. You take my word for it and stay away.'

'What kind of things?'

'Terrible things. Young Mark Foster's pet cat disappeared and his brother found it up by that house — dead!'

'How?'

'Nobody knows, there wasn't a mark on it. And I know others whose pets have gone missing lately.' The housekeeper, who had now broken two eggs into a frying pan and was splashing hot fat over them, turned to Liza and sighed deeply, 'Sacrifices . . . That's what they are!'

Liza shook her dark head unbelievingly and took another bite of her toast. Her mind shied away from Milly's implications, putting all that grisly nonsense down to local superstition, but the woman was adamant, muttering as she scooped the eggs onto a plate. 'It's dangerous up there, especially round that old house. No point walking into trouble.'

'By that old house I take it you mean Hazlehurst?'

'Aye, I do.'

'Why that place?'

'I'm saying no more! It doesn't do to talk about the devil.' Milly waddled back to the table, sitting down and wiping her hands on a cloth. 'That house is nothing but trouble, it has a curse on it and it's high time they pulled it down.'

'Who owns it?'

'It used to belong to the Forsythes but they've been long gone. Their last boy was killed in the war and nobody owns it now as far as I know. I heard someone had rented it but I don't know who they are. And, whoever they are, they must be mad, a body'd have to be daft — or up to no good — to stay in that place.'

Liza chuckled. 'Oh, Milly. Don't you think you're over-reacting a bit . . . ?'

'No! Just stay away, that's all. Now let's have another cup of tea and talk about something more cheerful. Look, here come Norman and Stevie, and the rain's stopped.'

Liza's heart went out to Stevie when he came into the kitchen, his face was drawn and white. He looked at her with such a sad expression in his dark eyes that he seemed to hold the weight of the world on his small shoulders. 'I can't find William,' he said, his voice quavering as he held back the tears. 'He wasn't here this morning when I got up and I don't know where he is.'

She made soothing sounds as she helped him off with his anorak, hoping she sounded more confident than she felt. 'He can't be far away, Stevie. He'll be back soon, you'll see.'

When Norman came in a few moments later, his own worry about the dog was equally plain, judging from the deep frown across his brow. 'He's not down by the river,' he commented, taking his boots off by the Aga. 'He must have gone onto the moor.' Norman was a tall man and only seemed smaller because his shoulders were stooped with the passing years. He was probably well into his seventies and yet there was still a lot of dark colour in his hair and beard. 'Don't worry, lad, he'll come back sooner or later when he's hungry.'

Stevie looked at Norman with eyes

full of hope. 'Do you think he has gone onto the moor, Norman? Can we go and look for him?'

'He can't be anywhere else. But you have to go to school, young Stevie . . . '

'But — '

Norman held up his hand, 'No buts, you can't miss school, William or no William. I'll go and look for him myself this afternoon.'

'I'll come with you,' said Liza, and the grateful smile from Stevie came straight from his heart.

After dropping him off outside the school, Liza and Norman set off to look for the dog and, in spite of the fact that she kept herself pretty fit, once out of the car she soon found Norman's pace exhausting.

There was no sign of William anywhere. Here and there a gorse bush still flowered even though it was so late in the year. No birds sang and they saw no-one. The only sounds for miles were her own anxious calls and the faint whistles from Norman as they fanned out across the moor.

After more than four hours they gave up the search. 'Stevie's going to be upset when he comes home from school and finds William still missing.' the old man muttered as they made their way back to Liza's car.

'I'll look again tomorrow.' Liza promised. 'I'm sure William can look after himself — another night on the moor won't hurt him, will it?'

'No, he's a tough old dog really. We'd better get back ourselves, though. Milly will be worrying.'

It was a disappointed pair who finally turned into the gates.

Later on, after supper, and when Stevie had gone fretfully to bed, Liza wished Anton would come home. She sat up until quite late waiting for him and, by midnight, when he still hadn't come back, Liza finally gave up and made her way upstairs.

Silently, she moved along the passage towards her room but at Stevie's door she paused, pressing her ear against the door and listening to the little boy's muffled, bitter sobs. After a few moments she could bear it no longer and went in.

Stevie raised his head from the pillow and looked at Liza with eyes red and swollen from weeping and, suddenly, she felt a quick rush of anger towards Anton. Where on earth had he gone? Was he still with Charity when he should be here to comfort his little boy? How could he think more of his cold, beautiful girlfriend when he should be here, with Stevie, his little boy who was heartbroken over his lost dog?

Liza moved quickly to the bed and sat down, reaching for Stevie and holding him close. 'Hush, hush, Stevie, don't cry . . . ' she murmured, ' . . . we'll find him, I promise.'

Stevie's dark eyes met Liza's with a frightened look. 'You don't think . . . '

Liza cupped his small face in her hands. His tone worried her, it held the unmistakable edge of fear. 'Think what, Stevie?'

His words tumbled out quickly. 'You don't think that the man's got him again, do you?'

Something cold gripped Liza's stomach. 'What man, Stevie? Tell me, what man?' But Stevie turned his head away quickly, a glimmer of tears starting again in his eyes. 'What man?' she urged again, 'Tell me, Stevie.'

'I wish Dad was here,' his voice quavered. 'He'd find William, wouldn't he?'

Liza stroked his fine hair and held him even closer, then Stevie swallowed and looked up into her face. 'Liza . . . can you keep a secret?'

'You know I can.'

'I think I know where William is . . .'

Liza wiped away the tears with the palm of her hand, his little cheeks hot and damp. 'Where would that be?'

Stevie gave a long, shuddering sigh. 'He'll — he'll be at the witches house — Hazlehurst. That was where I found him before. A man had tied him up,

120

a man with red hair . . . ' The little boy shivered as Liza held him. 'And, when I untied him, the man ran after me and tried to catch me.'

He looked up into Liza's face, fear, mingled with triumph shining in his eyes. 'He could never catch me! Me and William, we could run faster!' He bent his head low into his chest as he went on, his breath coming in sobbing gasps. 'But my dad was angry with me when I told him about it and he made me promise never to go near that house again. Dad says that man's not a very nice man.'

Liza cradled Stevie in her arms, somehow managing not to betray her acute unease. Her heart was touched with pity for this frightened little boy but her mind had gone racing back to her first day here, to the time she'd stopped on the moor and seen a red-haired man. Was it the same man? And was that place Hazlehurst — the witches house?

With shaking fingers she laid Stevie

down and tucked the covers cosily around him. 'If you're worried about the red-haired man stealing William again, then I'll go there first thing in the morning and look for him myself. I'll go to Hazlehurst and, if they've got him, then they'd better watch out.'

'Will you, Liza?' Stevie's face was chalk-white as his hand clutched her arm. 'Will you go to the house and see if he's there?'

Liza nodded firmly. 'I'll go first thing in the morning and I won't come back until I've found William, I promise.'

'And Dad can't get angry with you for going, can he, 'cos you're not a little kid like me, are you?'

Liza smiled, smoothing back the fine blonde hair, 'No, your dad can't get angry with me.'

Liza stayed with him until he'd fallen asleep, then switching off his light and tip-toeing out of the room, she went back to bed. Lying there, in the blackness, she suddenly felt very cold. What a rash promise she had made to

Stevie. The dog could be anywhere. The moor was a vast, barren wilderness and if he wasn't at the house she had no idea where else to start looking. Still, a promise was a promise and keep it she must, red-haired man or no red-haired man; witches or no witches.

Despite her conviction that she would never fall asleep, the next thing Liza was aware of was the pale sunlight playing on her eyes. When she went downstairs Milly was already up and dressed and layering rashers of bacon into the frying pan.

'You're up early,' she exclaimed as Liza came through the door. 'I'll just get Norman sorted out then I'll get you something to eat.'

'Just toast for me, and I'll do it,' she replied with a brightness she was far from feeling. 'Any sign of William this morning?'

'No, worse luck. That poor lamb is making himself ill with worry about it.'

'Is Anton back?'

Milly shook her head, 'No, not yet.'

After she'd eaten and despite Milly's protestations when she told her of her promise, Liza reached for her anorak. 'Well, I'm off now, wish me luck.'

'I don't like it, I don't like it one bit,' Milly muttered anxiously. 'Those moors are dangerous and I know Mr Anton will be furious when he finds out you've gone.'

Liza got into her car without any real plan in her head. She waved with feigned cheerfulness to the housekeeper as she drove through the gates, turning northwards, dropping into second gear as she made her ascent up the steep gradient. Ahead of her loomed the moors, grey and timeless and their peaks shrouded in drizzle.

Ten miles or so from the house the road became narrower. The craggy uplands of Brindle's Leap towered almost a thousand feet above sea level, filling Liza with a growing awareness of the desolation around her. It took her another hour to locate Hazlehurst, but there at last, she saw it. Half hidden between the great clefts of granite rock and scree lay the ram-shackle dwelling that had the power to put the fear of the devil into the people hereabouts.

She would have to make the rest of the way on foot, there was no way she could take the car any further. Liza switched off the engine and looked down. There was no sign of movement and with a sinking heart she began to feel that perhaps this search for William would turn out to be a complete waste of time.

Then she caught the gleam of an oblique light and she squinted towards it. Barely visible by the side of the house was a transit van and the light was coming from the sun on its wing mirror. Her heart beat a little faster. Should she walk openly up to the house and ask about the dog? Or should she play it safe and keep out of sight, bide her time to see what was going on? Liza decided she was going to take it easy and play it safe.

The descent to the house, however, was far from easy. The going was treacherous with the hidden slivers of shale, slippery as wet ice. She had almost reached what remained of the garden's wall when she stopped suddenly as the big looming shape of a man came from the side door of the house. He was barely three yards from her and she dropped quickly onto one knee, watching his movements from the concealment of the tangled undergrowth. Hardly daring to breathe, she saw him pass within touching distance, then he strode around the house towards the van.

He was young, about thirty, with a thicket of bright red hair, and his lips were puckered into a tuneless whistle. Liza felt the painful onset of cramp in her leg as she crouched and, when he had gone from sight, she peered back through the brambles towards the door. This time, she caught her breath! Standing there, unmistakable even in the shadow of the doorway, stood the elegant outline of Charity Gerhardt!

The man's voice called from the side of the house. 'Is that the lot?'

Charity answered him quickly, her voice tense and harsh. 'Keep your voice down, you fool! Someone may hear.'

Liza heard the sound of the van door closing, then the man appeared again. He walked up to the doorway and slipped his arms around Charity's waist. 'There's no-one for miles. Who can hear us here?'

'You never know . . . '

'I'll be glad when this lot's over with and we're away from this desolate awful place.'

Charity's cold laugh drifted to Liza's ears. 'It's served its purpose and, anyway, what have you to complain of?'

'I'm not complaining. But you know I don't like the way you've been throwing yourself at Demegar — even though it was necessary.'

Charity's laugh came again. 'Don't tell me you're jealous!'

The man's response was sulky. 'I've too much to think about to be jealous.'

'It's not your job to think, that's my department. You only have to do as you're told.'

They went back into the house and, when she heard the door close, Liza risked moving her position. She drew her cramped leg from under her, stretched it, only to sink to her knees again a moment later as they came out again. She fastened her eyes on the two people in the doorway, straining her ears to listen but their words were muffled as the man held Charity in a rough kiss.

Charity tweaked the man's check, 'Hold it, fella. Time enough for that when we're out of here.'

'I guess so.' The man's hands dropped to his sides and he bent to pick up a large blue case. 'What are we doing about the dog?'

Liza's heart began to race even faster now as Charity's reply reached her. 'He's all right. Barney's attending to that little matter tonight. I've given him a pill, he'll sleep for hours.'

'Why can't we get rid of him?'

The woman swung round to face the red-haired man, her green eyes bright and huge in their sockets and her wide mouth twisting grotesquely. There was a brisk authority about her that Liza had always suspected was there but had never seen. 'Will you leave things to me, Mitch, and stop trying to run the show?'

The man shrugged. 'I only thought — '

'You're not paid to think! Everything's arranged! Barney knows what to do!' She gave a harsh laugh as she added. 'If anyone is stupid enough to come looking for him, all they'll find is another . . . ' Charity paused, still making that harsh sound of a laugh. '*Sacrifice*. And good riddance to it!'

The man muttered something more as he pulled the door to and locked it, while Liza looked on in silent disbelief. At least Stevie's suspicions were confirmed now, and the dog they

129

referred to surely must be William. Crouched in her painful position she waited for them to move away, wondering what Anton had to do with all this. Did he know what his precious fiancee got up to behind his back? It was obvious now that Charity and this man called Mitch were on more than just speaking terms. And another thing struck her then. If Anton wasn't with Charity, as she'd suspected him of being, then where was he?

She hadn't time to speculate. She ducked her head lower as they passed to go to the van. They laughed softly together as they walked, and as they passed within inches, Liza heard Charity say, 'Well, at least, it's kept them away from here while we picked up the stuff.'

She waited until the van's engine had faded into the distance. They were using a road she hadn't known was there, and it was perhaps as well she hadn't, they would have seen her coming a mile off. When she felt it was safe to move she straightened up, looking warily over the rise in the direction they had taken. All was clear so, scrambling across the mound of old bricks that had once been the garden wall, she moved towards the house.

8

The door wouldn't budge as Liza pushed against it so she shouldered it again, harder this time. The hinges broke away from the lintel, weakening the frame; just one more push might do it. It took two or three in fact and her shoulder ached, but eventually the door splintered open and Liza found herself standing in a dark passage beneath a flight of stairs.

'*William*!'

There wasn't a sound. She moved along the passage towards another door, turning its handle. It gave way to her touch and, opening it, she looked around. It was filled with cardboard boxes, some labelled, 'FRAGILE', some unmarked, and, as she moved further into the room, she prised one open only to find that there was nothing inside except a few scrumpled oily rags.

An acrid smell assailed her nostrils, unsettling her stomach and making her turn back quickly into the passage. '*William! William! Where are you, boy?*'

The whole house had an eerie feel to it and Liza could well understand the local people's reluctance to come anywhere near this place. A prickly feeling chilled her spine as she moved around, looking first in one mouldy old room and then another.

At last, opening the final door at the end of the passage, she found herself face to face with the grim hearthstone of the old kitchen and it was then she heard the sound. It was so soft she could barely hear it and Liza stood stock still, listening hard, until it came again, louder this time. '*William?*'

She hadn't been mistaken. The pitiful sound of whimpering came from a recess beyond the fireplace and, instantly forgetting any fears she may have had, Liza rushed over to

133

it, stumbling a little on the raised stone flags of the floor. Reaching it she discovered yet another door and, thrusting against it again with her painful shoulder it gave way suddenly, disclosing a flight of stone steps leading downwards to a musty-smelling, poorly-lit cellar.

This time the whimpering sound was clear and Liza scrambled down the stairs. It was so dark she could hardly see and cursed herself for not having the sense to bring a torch, but at last, as her eyes grew accustomed to the darkness, she saw him.

'Oh, William, what have they done to you?'

Liza stumbled towards the un-mistakeable shape of Stevie's big black labrador. He was lying on a piece of filthy matting, a thick coil of rope attached to an iron ring on the wall and the other end tied around his collar.

'Oh, my goodness, what have they done?' she asked again, pulling on the rope around the iron ring. 'Come on, boy, I'm taking you home.'

It took a good ten minutes to loosen the tight knots but, when at last she managed it, the dog lurched to his feet, shaking himself and swaying unsteadily. Holding him now by the loose rope around his collar she led him, still groggy, up the steps and along the passage until they were once more out in the clean cold air of the moor.

Slowly and warily they made their way back to the car and Liza felt relieved to see that, as they climbed, William was making something of a recovery. She coaxed him on, almost weeping to see him looking so subdued and neglected, and a hot surge of anger welled up inside her at Charity's barbarous treatment of Stevie's beloved dog. They reached the car at last and giving William a helpful push, he half-leaped, half-stumbled onto the back seat. With a furious thrust of the gear-stick, Liza threw the car into reverse, edging away from the dry-stone wall and backing onto the road. As she turned the car back towards Daneshaw her dark eyes glittered. Never before had she been filled with such a feeling of burning anger and outrage!

There was still no sign of Anton when she arrived back at Lovell House, but Stevie's great whoop of joy when he saw William in Liza's car was worth all the effort she had put in to find him.

'I knew you'd find him, Liza!' he shrilled, grasping the handle of the car door to let out his beloved William. 'Come on, William, come on, boy, I'll ask Milly to find you a bone.'

They scampered off into the kitchen, Liza following behind to be met with Norman's grin of pleased relief. 'Where was he?'

'Where else?' replied Liza a little shortly. 'Hazlehurst.'

Milly butted in, her tone one of astonishment. 'Hazlehurst? I told you to keep away from there.'

Liza moved further into the kitchen, her colour high and her eyes still bright with her inner rage. 'I know you did, Milly, but what else could I do? It was a chance I had to take.' She lowered her voice so that Stevie couldn't hear as he ran in and out with the dog. 'And if you had seen the place they kept him — the conditions — ' Her voice quivered in temper. 'I'll tell you, Milly, if ever I get my hands on her, I swear I won't be responsible for my actions.'

Milly was staring wide-eyed. 'Get your hands on who?'

'On Charity Gerhardt, that's who!'

Milly's eyes opened even wider. 'Charity? Why Charity?'

'Because she's been the one behind it all.'

'But why?'

'I don't know, and she wasn't on her own in this either. She had someone to help with the dog-napping.'

'What do you mean?'

Liza turned exasperated eyes to the housekeeper. 'I mean, Milly, that Anton's precious fiancée has been

137

playing a few games of her own at that house. I saw them myself, Charity and a man with red hair ... A man called Mitch, I heard them say that they would get rid of William tonight — I was almost too late.'

Milly's hands flew to her face and she looked at Liza now through the tips of her fingers. 'Get rid of him? Do you mean — *kill him* . . . ?'

Liza nodded brusquely. 'Exactly.'

'Oh, the poor bairn! William was to be a sacrifice! Oh, the witches! The witches!'

'Milly, pull yourself together and make us all a cup of tea! Then I'll take a shower and get out of these filthy clothes.'

Half an hour later in the bathroom, Liza's fury sharpened itself against her sense of reason. What did Anton see in the woman anyway? It seemed she only had to crook her finger and he went running. Well, when he came home, she would have a few things to say to him about his bride-to-be!

Much later, when Stevie had gone with Norman to the stables and William was recovering from his ordeal by snoozing on his bean-bag by the Aga, Liza sat quietly in the sitting-room, turning things over in her mind. At the sound of Anton's car she glanced out to see him striding briskly across the drive, and even at that distance, she could see the haggard redness around his eyes. Liza went out into the kitchen to meet him and when he came through the door and saw her, he smiled in pleased surprise. 'Liza, am I glad to be home!'

He tossed his brief-case onto a chair, smiling again and waiting for her response. When it didn't come he eyed her quizzically, saying, 'I'm sorry I've had to leave you to your own devices for such a long time. Have you missed me?' He pursed his lips at her stony silence. 'What's the matter, lost your voice?' But his teasing smile froze as he recognised the murderous look on her face, his expression at once wary and guarded. 'What's happened? What's the matter?'

Liza turned away to look through the window, looking for the right words before she could tell him what was on her mind. She heard his impatient sigh behind her and turned back to face him.

Liza took a breath and began firmly. 'I wish I was a good liar, Anton, but I'm not. And I can't pretend any further that nothing needs to be said, so that's why what I'm going to say will sound so awful.'

Anton's expression showed no flicker of change. She paused for a moment, waiting for his reaction but, when none came, her chin went up and her eyes filled with grim determination. She told him the events of the last twenty-four hours. She told him of William's disappearance and of their search for him yesterday. She told him of Stevie's distress in the night and of the way she'd tried to comfort him, keeping her voice calm and steady as her emotions switched from sadness one moment to hot anger the next.

Liza paused for a moment, swallowing hard as she reached the point of telling him about her discoveries at Hazlehurst and it was then Anton at last spoke. The light from the window slanted across his face, sharpening the finely drawn angle of his cheek and jaw, his face set into a mask of poker-faced indifference. 'Where was he?' he asked flatly.

Liza gave him a hard look. My God, he was a cool one! 'I'm coming to that,' she said. 'But, before I do, I want to ask you something.'

Anton raised an eyebrow questioningly. 'I don't doubt that for a moment. What is it?'

'Who is the man with the red hair? The one they call Mitch?'

Anton's reaction was startling. It was sheer, speechless stupifaction and, as he stared at Liza, the old bitter look was on his face. Then he said, his tone curiously flat, 'Why do you ask me about him?'

'Because, whoever he is, he's the man who's scaring Stevie to death. He's the one who tried to steal William before, just as they tried to steal him this time.'

Anton's eyes, dark and withdrawn, were suddenly icy. '*They?*'

Liza felt herself tense up in the grip of decision. It had to come out now. She had to tell him of Charity's involvement — not only about Stevie's dog — but with the red-haired man as well. 'Yes . . . *They*. That's another thing I have to tell you. I found the dog at Hazlehurst and there's no doubt who was responsible for his disappearance. But it wasn't only the man . . . Charity is involved, too. I saw them.'

Anton seemed to be listening in a kind of frozen stillness that struck Liza as unnatural. Until she'd mentioned Hazlehurst he'd been watching her steadily, but now he'd glanced away. His eyes had narrowed and he fixed them on a point beyond her shoulder, saying nothing, and waiting for her to go on.

Suddenly everything came tumbling out of Liza. 'I don't know what sets your girlfriend apart from us lesser mortals. But she must have something that makes men fall over themselves for her! I just wish I knew what it was. She certainly doesn't feel any normal warmth towards anything else — and that covers children — and their pets!'

The scorn in Liza's voice increased as she told Anton of the conditions she'd found William in. All the time she was speaking, as her words spilled out, Anton listened without interruption. When, in the end, she fell silent, he remained still and calm, standing there in that strange, frozen attitude. Liza waited for him to speak but for a long time he said nothing, staring uneasily at the carpet with his head bent a little to one side. In that moment he looked, Liza thought, as though he could hardly stand for the weight of weariness, but then, suddenly, his eyes lifted and Liza felt her heart jolt at the cold expression in them.

'Did they see you?' he asked very quietly.

She stiffened. 'Is that all you have to say?'

'*DID THEY SEE YOU*?' he asked again, louder this time.

Liza felt the icy grip take hold of her heart.

'No, I don't think so. But they'll soon realise someone was there. It won't take this Barney fellow long to work out that the dog has gone and the door was forced. And there's something else . . .'

'Still more?'

'Yes, and you're going to like this even less.'

'I doubt it.'

Liza paused for a moment, breathing deeply. Then, keeping her voice as even as she could, she said, 'It's about Charity — I have to say it.'

144

He held her expression coldly. 'Yes?'

'I don't think she's — ' Liza's chin went up. 'I don't think she's good enough to be a mum for Stevie, he's much too sweet and fine a boy to be placed into her dubious care!'

There, she'd said it! It was done! She felt as though someone had slapped her face and woken her feelings in the most unpleasant way. She hated the fact that she was interfering like this, but what else could she do?

Liza fell silent and waited. Anton had straightened up to his full height and turned cold, expressionless eyes towards her but, when he next spoke, his words cut through her like a knife.

'*You're to leave this house right away!*'

Liza stared in disbelief. She knew her words would anger him, but she hadn't bargained on a reaction like this — that he would demand she leave the house. Yet, looking at him now, she knew he meant every word and a cold, hard knot tightened inside her chest.

Squaring her shoulders, she faced him full on. 'Very well, if that's what you want. I'll leave at the end of the week.'

Anton turned away abruptly, opening the door and throwing her such a pent-up look that she almost uttered a cry of alarm. Then he rasped in a voice sounding like cracked ice, *'No, that won't do! I want you out of here first thing tomorrow morning.'*

Without another word he left the room, leaving the door wide-open and Liza staring after him in wide-eyed shock. For a long time she didn't move, frozen where she stood, then slowly gathering herself she made her way upstairs, reeling in a wave of hot anger at the man who had so utterly and completely shattered her.

In her room, her head resting against the heavy folds of the curtain, she watched Anton's movements as Stevie came back into the garden with Norman. He scooped him up into his arms and held him close, his mouth forming words that caused his little son to hug him closer.

Bewildered, Liza watched them. It was a poignant moment and, in spite of everything, Liza felt as though her heart would break in two for love of them. A wave of compassion flooded through her, a wave so physical, so real, that it left her shaking. She watched them a few moments longer until, still carrying Stevie in his arms, Anton turned and came back into the house.

Liza turned away, reaching for her suitcase and tossing it onto the bed. Hot tears scalded her eyes at the injustice of it all. He was dismissing her as though she was some nineteenth-century governess without a friend to her name. Well, he was wrong about that at least! She had friends! And she wouldn't wait until morning, she would leave tonight! She would pack her things and go back to Megan while she still held on to a vestige of pride.

The phone rang by her bed, jerking her bitter thoughts back to the present, and when she picked it up Milly's voice told her she would bring up a tray.

'Don't bother, Milly, I couldn't eat a thing,' Liza told her, the thought of food choking her.

But Milly was adamant and a few minutes later a knock at the door told Liza her tray had arrived.

'The door's open, Milly,' she called, bending over her case, 'Put the tray on the table, will you? I'll eat it later,' she added, keeping her face averted in the effort to hide her misery from the housekeeper.

'It's me, Liza.'

She spun round at the sound of Anton's voice. He was the last person she expected to see. 'Anton, what on earth . . . '

His eyes swept the room. 'Just checking to see if your passport's up to date.'

Liza's mouth dropped open. 'My passport?'

'Is it?'

'What do you mean?'

Anton sighed resignedly. 'I mean
. . . Is your passport still in order?'

'Yes, but why?'

'Because you're going to need it. I'm
taking you away in the morning, you
and Stevie.'

Liza felt her knees turn to jelly as
she sat down quickly on the edge of
the bed, looking up at Anton in sheer
astonishment. 'Taking me away?' she
asked faintly.

'Yes, I'm afraid it's become necessary.'

'Where are you talking me — us?'

Anton came to sit beside her on
the bed, taking her hand gently in
his, squeezing it in gentle reassurance.
'We're going to my place in France.'

'France?'

'Yes, I have a small place by the
Loire at Ecouflant, a few miles south
of Angers. You should be safe there.'

Liza was finding her voice again,
suddenly she felt very alert. 'Safe?'

Anton nodded his dark head. 'Yes,
safe.' His voice was deceptively casual
and for a moment Liza felt a vague

sensation of alarm.

'Safe from what, Anton? What is this danger you see for me? Perhaps, if you told me, I could recognise it for myself.'

But Anton shook his head. 'No, I don't think you would, and you may not even be in danger,' that old familiar edge crept back, ' . . . but I'm taking no chances.'

Liza gave a small shake of her head. Things were moving too fast for her to take them in lucidly, and the slight pressure of Anton's hand on hers was already affecting her more than she dared admit. 'But I thought . . . ' she murmured.

He glanced quickly at her, 'Thought what?'

She let out a long breath. 'I thought you were sending me away because of what I said about Charity.'

At that Anton laughed bitterly. 'Is that the kind of man you think I am? The kind who would send you away because you cared for my son?'

'I'm afraid I hardly know what to think.'

Anton took both of Liza's hands in his. 'Liza, this may surprise you, but I love Stevie more than I can say. You surely don't doubt that, do you?'

'No, I don't doubt that at all.' Her mind flashed back to the scene she had witnessed in the garden only a little while ago, and of the tender love which shone between father and son. 'But, Anton . . .'

'Ssh . . . Please, Liza. No more questions tonight, there isn't time, I have a lot of things to do.' Liza studied his face, noting the strong character lines that etched it and the implacable set of his mouth. His eyes roved across her face, lingering on her mouth. 'These last few weeks have been hell,' he whispered. 'I haven't been able to stop myself from thinking of you . . .'

'But, Anton . . . Charity — '

'Don't force me, Liza, leave it alone.'

She pulled away a little, chilled by

his response, 'How can I leave it alone?'

Anton pulled her back, holding her close and kissing her deeply. When they came up for air his voice was no more than a throaty whisper. 'There is a reason, trust me. You can't believe I could love that self-centred iceberg? Surely you know me better than that?'

Liza shook her head slowly. In that moment she didn't even care. Her deep need for Anton flared up inside her, quickening her breathing and setting her soul alight.

He pulled himself up, caressing her cheek with a stroke of his hand, then, kissing her once more he crossed the room to the door, turning and saying, 'When you're packed come downstairs for a bite to eat. By then I should have the route organised with the airport and all the weather reports.' Then, blowing her a kiss, he left.

Liza stood by the window, hugging her arms around her waist. The sky was bright with stars now and she had never seen them look so extraordinarily big. Tomorrow she would be in France! It was unbelievable! Charity was forgotten for the moment. And so too was the aura of danger that Anton carried so heavily about him. These special moments were precious and rare. And even if they only lasted for tonight, it would surely be enough.

9

It was pandemonium in the kitchen when she went downstairs the next day. Norman was packing William's things into a cardboard box and Stevie, in spite of his ordeal of the last two days, was helping him and showing no sign of tiredness.

'Had Dad told you where we're going, Liza?' he called excitedly as she came in.

'Yes, he has,' Liza replied, eyeing the box dubiously and adding, 'don't tell me William's coming with us, too?'

'No.' Stevie shook his blond head reflectively, his frown betraying his disappointment. 'Dad says he would have to spend ages in qua-qua-quarantine so Norman's taking him to Uncle Tommy's till we come back.'

'Better safe than sorry,' muttered Milly. 'If that snooty piece tries to harm him again, she'll get more than she bargained for with our Tommy!'

After breakfast, and with Milly's tearful goodbyes still ringing in their ears, they set off for the airport. In next to no time, Anton was leading them through the brisk bustle of the commercial aircraft and towards the silver and blue of his private plane — a small executive Lear. Surely, she would wake up soon! This wonderful, emotional, pink bubble she found herself in was far too good to last and, as the plane took off, she sent up a little prayer. Please, don't burst my bubble yet . . . Not just yet . . .

Over the English Channel, Anton left the flying to the automatic pilot and came through the cabin door. He disappeared momentarily into the galley, only to emerge a few minutes later with a bottle of champagne and two glasses. He placed them on the pull-down table and reached up to the luggage rack, lifting down a flower which he handed to Liza with a gallant flourish. It was a single white rose.

'Happy birthday to my Yorkist lady!'

Liza gasped. She had completely forgotten today was her birthday and, looking at Anton with eyes as wide as saucers, she laughed in happy surprise. 'Well, thank you, Anton, this is all . . . ' she shook her head as she ran out of words and took the rose, breathing in its fragrance and smiling broadly.

'Fancy a drop of bubbly to celebrate?'

He filled her glass with the sparkling wine and Liza sipped at it in heady amazement. One thing was for sure, she thought, with a definite realisation, the more she grew to know him, the more surprising he became.

He eased himself down into the seat by her side. 'I can't join you, I'm afraid. Drinking and flying don't mix! My part in the celebration will have to wait until I come to you at 'La Chesnaie' — that's the name of my place,' he explained, anticipating her question. 'I'll have to get back to the flight-deck soon so I'll fill you in quickly about the arrangements.'

'But aren't you coming to the villa with us?'

He shook his dark head. 'I can't — not right away. I have to get back. But I've arranged for a friend of mine to meet you. He's an American — Smithy. He'll pick you up at the airport and stay with you at the villa.' Anton grinned at her perplexed expression, adding more somberly, 'Be sure to do everything he says, he knows the score.'

Confused, Liza nodded her agreement. 'If you say so, but when will I see you again?'

'Very soon. I have some business to see to first, then I have to be in Paris by Wednesday. I should be with you in about a week — '

'Dad . . . '

Stevie's plaintive call interrupted him and Anton looked down the aircraft at his son. 'What is it?'

'Can I have a go at the controls?' Stevie, who had been at the other end of the plane pretending to be Captain

Kirk, came running up now to make sure his father remembered his vow. 'You *did* promise . . . '

'All right,' Anton grinned. 'But when I tell you to come back to your seat I want no argument, OK?'

'OK.'

Anton got up and turned to look at Liza. 'We should be landing at Nantes in just under an hour.' He laid a reassuring hand on hers, smiling softly. 'Remember, stick close to Smithy until I can get there, promise?'

Liza smiled back, knowing this was not the time for any questioning, and answered, 'Promise.'

When the two of them withdrew to the flight-deck, Liza stroked Anton's rose along her cheek. Below her lay the sun-steeped fields of France, glowing now like living gold, and the lazy, sliding silver of the river Loire reflected its light under the lace-like spans of bridges. A few minutes later, when Stevie returned to his seat, came Anton's voice, 'Fasten your seatbelts, we're coming into Nantes.'

Anton guided them through the hurly-burly of the airport reception, raising his hand in recognition as a man strode up to meet them. 'Hi, Smithy, good to see you.'

Liza was bemused as she went through the introductions. The man looked in his mid-twenties, immensely tall, and as black as jet. His jeans were old and frayed below the 'IT'S ME BEHIND HERE' logo on his T-shirt, and beneath the green and gold woollen bob-cap fell the orange-tinted dreadlocks of a Rastafarian.

'Hey, man,' he drawled, his face split into the widest smile she had ever seen. 'Welcome to France, we'll sure have a dance!' Then, turning his friendly grin to Liza and pumping her hand, he said, 'Winston Churchill Smith at your service — but don't take pity, you call me Smithy!' He picked up their cases in one easy movement, continuing in his odd way of communication. 'I'll take the bags that carry your rags, and we'll go on to Chesnaie, where I hope you'll make hay!'

Anton, once he was certain that they were safe in Smithy's care, and after a few last brief words in the man's ear, left them, vanishing quickly through the crowds and back to his plane. Strangely, Liza felt suddenly very safe, walking behind Smithy's massive physique and listening to Stevie's giggling chatter.

Anton's villa was superb. It lay in an enchanting spot, surrounded by tall mature trees and just a stone's throw from the sun-dappled banks of the beautiful river Loire. She even sang to herself when Smithy had shown her up to her room and, as she stepped out onto the balcony that overlooked a shaded courtyard, she felt in a mood of pleasant weariness. It was later, much later, when they'd eaten and Stevie was curled up asleep in his room, that Liza lay in the half-world of sleep and wakefulness and thought of Anton. She turned her head to look at the white rose by her bedside and at the moonlit shadow it was throwing across the room, and she wondered . . . Had Anton ever brought Charity here?

The next few days were wonderful. They lazed about the river bank, sometimes swimming and sometimes fishing. They went for long walks or played tennis. In fact they did most of the things that mark a normal, pleasant holiday. It was only after three or four days that Liza realised Smithy never left their side, sticking to them like a limpet.

But then the bubble burst!

On the fifth day, Liza was stretched out on a lounger by the pool, half-reading, half-dozing, and glancing now and then at Stevie as he played in the water. For the first time since they'd arrived in France, Stevie and Liza were alone. Smithy had gone into Angers for more supplies and left them with the strict instructions they were on no account to leave the villa until he got back.

Now, chillingly, a shadow fell over

her page and suddenly a tight knot wrapped itself around Liza's heart as she looked up. It seemed to stop in mid-beat as she recognised the woman standing so elegantly above her, the green eyes staring down, cold, unsmiling. It was Charity Gerhardt!

At last Liza stirred, swinging her legs off the lounger to face her unwelcome visitor. Everything had grown quiet and silent and, Stevie, recognising the woman straight away, climbed quickly out of the pool and Liza felt his cold little hand creep into her own.

The beautiful face broke into a brittle smile and Charity's clipped accent came across to Liza like silvers of ice. 'You look surprised to see me, Liza!'

Liza regarded Charity with her dark eyes full of wary curiosity. 'Surprised? Yes, I am. What do you want, Charity? What are you doing here?'

The woman's eyes were mocking now and her twisted little smile turned Liza's heart to stone. 'I don't have to give you my reasons.' Charity let out that cold insincere laugh of hers and Liza's heart leaped into her throat at the undisguised hatred in the glittering emerald eyes.

'I think you do,' Liza answered coldly. 'And I'm asking you again, why are you here?'

The woman sighed in annoyance. 'Very well, if you insist. This place does belong to Anton, doesn't it?'

'You know it does.'

'Then I've every right to be here — and you must go.'

Liza felt like a block of stone. She knew instinctively that something was wrong — very wrong, and whatever that something was, her idyllic days here were over. She tried to keep her voice controlled but it was difficult. 'What do you mean, I must go?'

'Anton and I were married two days ago — in Paris. You surely wouldn't want to play gooseberry on our honeymoon, would you?'

Liza heard Stevie's small cry beside her. The breeze blowing across the river was lifting Charity's silver hair from her face and suddenly Liza felt faint. The woman was lying — she had to be! Anton and Charity married! Never! The courtyard seemed to have suddenly metamorphosed into a living creature, suffocating Liza in its ominous silence. She could hear her own breath raking in her lungs and an icy coldness take possession of her.

She steadied herself, gripping the back of the lounger with her free hand. 'You're lying!'

Charity's cold laugh reached her unbelieving ears. 'Why should I lie? And now you'll have to go, we don't want you here. There's a plane for England at six o'clock, and I want you to be on it.'

Liza's dark eyes glistened like frost. 'I'm not leaving!'

'You have no choice. As Anton's wife, I'm ordering you to.'

Liza's panic was ebbing away now and in its place came a determination to hold her ground. 'My orders come

164

from Anton, and until he tells me to leave, I'm staying here — with Stevie.'

Charity took a step toward her. 'You will do as I say,' she spat, her voice broken in its hatred.

Liza shook her head stubbornly. 'I will do as Anton says.' A hot surge of anger lifted her and cleared her thoughts. There was no way she would leave Stevie alone with Charity Gerhardt, she didn't trust the woman an inch. 'We'll wait and see what he tells me to do.'

'Is she being difficult?'

Both women spun round at the man's voice and Liza's heart sank even more as she recognised Charity's red-haired friend, Mitch, standing by the sun-lounge door. It was the first time she'd seen him this close and his heavy-lidded eyes regarded her menacingly as he stood there, his hands thrust deep into his trouser pockets.

'I guess you could say that,' Charity answered him, triumph edging into her voice. 'You couldn't have come at a better time.'

The man stepped forward. 'Time's going on. We can't waste any more on her. Vasquez has already spoken to the boss, we have to be at Cap Renou by four — he'll meet us up there.'

'Right, let's get on with it!' Suddenly, Charity lunged forward, grabbing Stevie by his arm and Liza, hearing his yell, threw herself between them, hitting out wildly. She grabbed the American by the shoulder, thrusting her away, but before she could pull Stevie towards her, she heard a rushing, whistling noise behind her, fast and unexpected. She felt the pain, and a sharp searing sensation piercing the back of her head. A million coloured lights spun and circled before her eyes, and the last thing she heard as she sank into oblivion was, 'No, leave her, you fool! Quick! Get the boy!'

★ ★ ★

Something cool was pressed against her head and Liza felt the comfort of encircling arms around her. A voice was willing her back to consciousness and, squinting up dully, she saw Smithy's dark, troubled eyes searching her face.

'Smithy . . . ' she began. 'What's happened?' Then, as realisation dawned, she sat up with a start, the sudden movement starting her head throbbing again and dull mists clouding her mind. 'Smithy . . . !' Liza clutched at his sleeve. 'Stevie! My God, they've taken Stevie!'

'You must tell me what happened, Liza,' he urged. 'It's vital! Do you feel up to it?'

She nodded. 'Yes. I'm all right. It was Charity. She was here — '

Liza forced her mind to work and told him, starting at the point where Charity came in and ending with the blow Mitch had dealt her. According to her watch she must have been out cold for almost fifteen minutes and they could have taken Stevie anywhere

167

by now. Smithy straightened up, his eyes revealing a hard look.

'They mentioned a place.' Liza commented. ' 'Cap Renou' — do you know it?'

'Yes, I know it,' Smithy gritted his teeth, adding quietly, 'Liza, I have to go. Now you take it easy after that crack on the head and, whatever you do, wait here, until either Anton or I get back, OK?'

'What's going on, Smithy? Can I come with you?'

'No, it's dangerous enough as it is.' And, without another glance in her direction, he ran round the side of the house to a dust-covered army jeep.

Liza stood undecided. Then, impetuously following her instincts, she ran to the garage and jumped into Anton's 2CV. Her face was grim and her head still ached, but she didn't care. Whatever was going on it was time she found out for herself. Doggedly, she thrust her foot down on the accelerator, heading in the direction of Angers, keeping Smithy's jeep about a mile ahead.

Once through Angers, on the metalled main road to the south, Smithy increased his speed and Liza was hard-pressed to keep up with him, until, five miles beyond Angers he turned off onto a minor road, curving and zig-zagging like a switch-back. She pulled up sharply, braking when she saw that Smithy had stopped in the drive by high trees so dense that she almost missed him.

Liza jerked her car into a grove of trees, distancing herself about two hundred yards away. She hadn't a clue what to do next and sat very still, trying to formulate some kind of plan. After a few minutes she got out and made her way carefully towards the chateau, making sure that the trees concealed her presence.

She reached the house, skirting along its length until she heard muffled sounds coming from one of the open windows and, peering through, it was then she saw Anton. Charity's voice reached her ears, and listening hard, she realised that the subject of their conversation was herself.

'She's a fool — and now she's dangerous. Supposing she goes to the police? She could ruin everything!'

'I told you to let me see to her.'

'I tell you she doesn't know a thing,' Anton spoke now and Liza pressed her ear even closer to the frame. 'I sent her here for a holiday, that's all. How was I to know the arrangements were to be transferred here?'

The voices became muffled again as they moved around the room and Liza couldn't hear anymore. Her heart raced as she stood there wondering what to do. Should she go to the police? There was still time. But what could she tell them?

But then Liza heard something else! The door at the front of the house suddenly burst open and, craning her neck to see what was happening now, her heart gave a sudden lift as Stevie came running through, yelling and pointing excitedly to the sky. Suddenly, the air was filled with police sirens and the whirl of helicopters and, within seconds, pandemonium seemed to break loose.

Liza ran stumbling forward towards Stevie, so glad to see that he was unharmed but, before she could reach him, she came face to face with a small army of policemen and men dressed for combat. And then, as the door of the chateau opened again, she almost cried out as she saw Anton. But suddenly she stopped in her tracks because, when her senses cleared, she saw that his arm was around Charity, holding her closely, and his other arm around someone else — a girl! The girl she'd seen in the photograph, and the girl she'd seen in the church. It was his sister, Elizabeth!

He opened one of the cars and ushered Charity in, holding the other girl by the hand and calling out to one of the men, 'You timed that well,

Mike! It was nearly too late.'

Mike! At last!

Liza's eyes flew towards the man who had come up to embrace Anton warmly and what she saw almost made her legs buckle beneath her. It was her brother, Charlie!

Reeling with shock she retreated back to the side of the house, needing space to breathe and time to think. Seeing her brother, and Anton's close proximity to Charity had paled everything in her mind into insignificance. So it was her brother who was a part of this! He and Anton were involved in something that was surely against the law! Otherwise, why all the secrecy — and now all the police?

She thanked God that Stevie was safe, but what to do next was an ever bigger problem! A part of her was numb and, as her sandals crunched against the gravel of the drive, she felt she had to have some time on her own.

Liza reached her car at last, fumbling

172

in her shorts pocket for the key. Wearily, she climbed in, pressing her foot on the clutch and reaching for the gear-stick.

'Don't yell out and you won't get hurt!'

The man's words were sharp with impatience and, in that moment, Liza knew that her ordeal was far from over.

10

Liza tried to turn round, but her head wouldn't move. The voice from the back seat was all too familiar and, although she couldn't see his face, she knew that the man was Anton's friend, Hugo Stout.

'What do you want with me?' Somehow her question tumbled out, but her jaw was stiff, compacted, making it almost impossible to breathe let alone move.

'You're my insurance — my ticket out of here,' he grated. 'Now get moving! And drive normally — as though nothing was wrong!' When Liza made no move he pressed the cold nozzle of an automatic pistol hard against the back of her head. 'You heard me! Start the car!'

'The police are everywhere. You'll never — '

'Be quiet! Keep your mouth shut or I'll shut it for you!'

His threat spurred Liza into action. She headed back towards the road, stealing a quick glance in the mirror at the man behind. He sat low in the seat, his head pressed back against it and his indolent eyes glinting with an urgency of purpose.

'You'll never get away with this. They'll . . . '

'Stop talking and drive, will you! And stay on this road. Keep off the autoroute.'

He moved his position so that the gun pressed against the nape of her neck and Liza fell silent. There was nothing she could do, so she drove on southwards, the dust streaming out behind them and the car rattling over the uneven ribbed surface.

Five miles on Liza glanced at the fuel gauge and realised that the needle was flickering on EMPTY. She hadn't bothered to check it when she'd set out so recklessly for Cap Renou. And it could only be a matter of a few miles before the last of it was gone. She pressed hard on the accelerator, taking the next bend with such a jerk that the impact sent the car veering to the right in a sickening swerve. Hugo yelled as the swerve sent him off balance, but she hadn't managed to dislodge his grip on the gun.

Another two miles and the road switched sharply left and, through a blur, Liza saw her chance. The verge banked sharply and, unhesitatingly, she pointed the car towards a gap — a cart track — the edge of the slope leaping towards the wheels. Again, Liza took the car into a swerve, but this time she was in earnest.

'Slow down, you fool! Are you crazy?'

But Liza wasn't listening now. She jerked the wheel and thrust her foot down on the brake. The back of the car swung round in a left-handed skid, swinging off the road and plunging crazily onto the slope. The impact was enough to send Hugo flying across the back seat as the offside wheels hit another jut of rock. Then they were bumping over the rough grass of open land, sparse vegetation dancing around them and Liza, flicking a tongue over her dry lips, felt a spurt of blood.

But she was also feeling good. She twisted away from another wedge of rock, the car missing it by inches, and then it juddered to a stop on the clumpy uneven ground — the petrol tank was empty. It was now or never! Grabbing the handle of the door Liza flung it open, swinging her legs round as a powerful survival instinct took over.

'Are you crazy? You almost killed us!' The man's voice was ugly as he threw himself forward to grab her. 'Get back into the car!'

A bullet clipped a nearby boulder as Liza ran for her life and, for one terrifying moment, she felt sure that he would finish her off there and then. She ran even faster, not looking back, but she knew he wasn't far behind. The breath was rasping through her lungs, fear rising in her throat as she felt him gaining on her, causing her to cry out, 'Help me! Somebody help me!'

Liza made for the cover of the trees, praying for a farmhouse, but there was nothing she could see and she knew she couldn't keep this pace up much longer.

Then, however, the sound of a helicopter clattered overhead and she heard a disembodied voice calling, 'Freeze, Stout! Leave the girl alone, you're going nowhere!'

Liza felt his hand grab at her arm, and pull her back as she kicked out in blind panic. She cried out, pushing against him for dear life until a crippling stitch made her stop and bend forward in agony. That was all he needed. In seconds he grabbed her, his breath rasping against her ear. 'Stop playing Wonder Woman — you're my insurance. Why do you think you're still alive?'

Liza fought for breath and still tried to twist away. They were under the trees now and a feeling of suffocation swept over her as he lunged forward, bringing her down and making any further attempt to escape impossible.

'Don't you dare lay a finger on me,' she gasped, her eyes flashing fire and her entire body tightened into instantaneous reflex.

Her cry fell on deaf ears. 'Relax, pretty girl, if you're good enough for Demegar, you're good enough for me.'

There was a malevolence in his voice that terrified her. He lunged across her clumsily and his mouth came down onto her face, hot, loose and sickening. She turned her head into his upper arm, avoiding contact with the man's hideous mouth, and then, with overwhelming savagery, she sank her teeth into the soft fleshiness of his upper arm.

He yelled, high-pitched like a child, 'Stop that or I'll break your neck!'

But Liza had already pulled herself away and started to run. Only one thing was in her head now, she had to somehow signal the helicopter.

Strange sounds came from behind as she stumbled forward. She heard someone calling her name, 'LIZA!' and somewhere, a long way away, she swore she heard the sound of a car. A car! Someone to help her at last!

Sanity came back to her as she ran towards the blurred figures just a few yards away. The grogginess was falling away with the reality that help was at hand at last. 'Liza here! Over here!'

She turned, trying to think clearly, seeing a familiar figure with his arms outstretched to catch her as she pitched towards him. His face was as white as chalk and Liza felt the firm grip of his arms as she fell into them. 'Thank heavens you're all right!'

She clung onto her brother, choking with relief, 'Oh, Charlie . . . Charlie . . .' Then she saw the two running figures a few yards away. She saw Anton and Hugo Stout, and she saw Anton hurl himself at the other man's legs, bringing him down in a tackle that would have floored any rugby player. She watched them, baffled by what was happening, as they wrestled and fought over the course earth.

Anton threw himself straddle-legged across Hugo and grabbed his arm, twisting it across his back and forcing him onto his stomach. He gave the arm another vicious twist that brought a scream-like sound from the man beneath him. 'That's my farewell gift for you, Hugo!' Anton rasped, glancing across to Liza and her brother. 'Charlie! Liza! One of you get the gun!'

They ran towards him, Liza spotting the gun where Hugo had dropped it in the struggle. She threw herself forward, snatching it up and tossing it to Anton who drove the nozzle hard into Stout's back, straightening up but not loosening his hold. 'OK, you can get up now, it's all over.'

Hugo's mouth was twisted into the semblance of a smile as he dragged himself up but, in spite of the smile, he was visibly shaken as he scowled at Anton. 'I knew I was right about you, Demegar — it was never your style.' Then he turned to Charlie, 'And you, Mike, you're one of them, too?'

He laughed bitterly. 'You really took us in.' Hugo Stout put his head a little to one side, eyeing Charlie with unsuppressed hatred. 'We screened you with a fine tooth comb and came up with nothing. My compliments to your people — you really had us fooled.'

Anton waved the gun, indicating for Hugo to start walking. 'Move, Stout, before I'm tempted to save the taxpayers a quid or two.'

Two policemen stepped up, slipping handcuffs around his wrists and leading him towards the helicopter. Liza, Charlie and Anton didn't stir for at least three minutes, watching the swirl of dust as the helicopter hovered above them, until finally, Charlie said, 'Well, I guess that's it. We can all go home.'

A small breeze blew across Liza's

cheek and she felt Anton's hand in the small of her back, guiding her along the field. She threw him an anxious glance, 'Anton, where's Stevie now?'

'He's fine. He's gone back to the villa with Smithy.' Anton gave a low chuckle. 'I don't think he's ever going to stop telling his pals about this — he thinks he's had a great adventure.'

They walked on. Liza felt too tired to lift her head, but she braced herself for her next, inevitable question. 'And Charity . . . ?'

'What about Charity?'

'Is she back at the villa, too? I hear congratulations are in order.'

Anton stopped, his hand on Liza's arm. Then he turned her to face him, a puzzled frown on his face. 'Why?'

Liza swallowed, looking up, 'On your marriage . . . '

Incredulity swept across his face as he stared down at her. 'My marriage? Are you kidding me?'

'I'm not kidding anyone — that's what she told me. She told me you were married when you were in Paris.'

He turned his astonished eyes to Charlie and then back to Liza. 'You surely didn't believe her, did you? It's just not true!'

'Then why should she say it?'

'Because she's a vicious, sick person,' this last remark came from Charlie. 'Perhaps she thought that was the only way to get you back to England and out of her way. She loves to hurt. It's the kind of sick ploy a woman like that would use. But you can forget her, and her buddy, Mitch. Anton held onto her like a clamp until the police took over. They should be well on the way to Paris by now — and to prison for their part in all this.'

So Anton was putting the woman in police custody when he stuck so close to her at the chateau! He was making sure she didn't get away! Liza felt the lump rise in her throat. An overwhelming feeling of relief and love flooded over her but, even now, she knew she had to ask, 'But, Anton, you

184

were engaged to her, I heard you say so myself.'

A sombre expression fell across his face, softened by a tenderness that threatened to break her heart. 'I had no choice. I had to gain her confidence and that seemed to be the only way.' He gave a quick intake of breath and went on softly, 'I couldn't explain — not then. But you must know by now how I feel about you.'

Charlie cleared his throat discreetly. 'If you'll excuse me, I'll leave you two to sort this out and meet you back at the car.' He leaned forward and kissed Liza lightly on her cheek, adding as he moved away, 'Don't blame Anton, Liza. It was all my idea — I asked him to go along with it.'

When Charlie had gone Anton pulled her towards him, his eyes serious and tender. 'I'm sorry I couldn't tell you before, it would have ruined everything. But, more than that, I didn't want you involved. When you hear the full story, I know you'll see why. For the moment, that's not important. What is important is that you know how I feel. I love you, Liza — I can tell you at last. And — I've been hoping that you could learn to love me too.'

For the first time, without restraint, a ray of hope shone bright and free, open and honest, and she uttered the words she thought she would never be allowed to say. 'I love you, too, Anton. I think I've loved you from the first day of my life.'

He held her in a kiss that almost took her breath away, his lips feathering across her eyelids and along her cheek. His voice was husky as he whispered her name, 'Liza, oh, Liza, what a fool I've been.'

'You're no fool, Anton.'

'Yes, I am, for hiding my love from you. How long does it take for two people to realise how much they love each other?'

Liza smiled slowly, 'It's not how long it takes, it's how long they both need to admit it.'

'Perhaps.' He laughed and kissed her again, then pulled away from her gently, reluctantly, a small wry smile playing around the corners of his mouth. 'We'd better move, my love, before I get carried away. Look, Charlie's still waiting. If he wasn't, I'm sure I'd keep you here in this field forever.'

Smiling together and holding hands, they moved on. As they drew nearer to her brother, Liza became acutely conscious of Anton's car lying drunkenly on the slope just a few yards away.

'You made a good job of my Citroen,' she heard him remark as they neared it. 'What were you trying to do? Get some practice in for Le Mans?'

Liza threw him a rueful glance. 'I ran out of petrol.'

'Silly thing to do.'

Liza nodded her agreement with a wry grin. 'Yes, and a good thing for me that I did. But how did you know where to find me?'

Anton's eyes were bleak. 'We didn't

at first and it scared me, you've no idea how much! We knew you could be in danger when Smithy came for Stevie, leaving you alone at the villa. The meeting at Cap Renou was set up to collar the top man in their organisation and, when Hugo didn't show, we knew our suspicions were right about him.'

'Charity, Mitch and Barney Vasquez were small fry — we could have picked them up any time. It was the chief we wanted and we hoped, by setting up a deal for the biggest consignment they'd ever handled, Hugo wouldn't be able to resist it; that he'd come into the open and give himself away.'

Liza looked at him steadily. 'But he didn't, did he? What went wrong?'

'He'd found out that I wasn't who I said I was. That's also why he got Mitch and Charity to snatch Stevie — to keep me toeing the line until he could get his hands on the money.'

They reached Charlie's car and climbed in, Liza sitting in the back. Her brother took up the story now as Anton drove. 'When the search for Hugo started, Anton got worried when he knew you were alone at the villa. He telephoned, but you weren't there so we put two and two together — that, somehow, Hugo had got hold of you, to use you as a means of escape.'

'We didn't realise you'd come out to Cap Renou as well, though. Hugo must have spotted you and made his break. We searched the area from the helicopters and spotted Anton's CV. You know the rest from there, Liza.'

Liza held herself perfectly still, looking first at Charlie and then at Anton. 'That's just the point,' she said quietly, 'I still don't know a thing. Who are you all? What have you been involved in? I wish somebody would just tell me what's been going on!'

Anton glanced at Charlie and then grinned ruefully, 'It's a long story, Liza, but I promise, I'll explain everything when we get back to Le Chesnaie.'

Later that night, when Anton and Liza had tucked a happy Stevie into bed and they had come back to the dining-room, Liza looked around at the three people sitting at the table into whose lives she had so innocently stumbled. There was a deep silence, and in that silence Liza heard herself say, 'Well, any volunteers? Elizabeth? Charlie? Anton?'

Anton nodded his head, taking a sip of wine, swallowing slowly and then saying softly, 'You've waited long enough, my love. It's time we told you what's really been going on. Charlie, do you want to start?'

Charlie smiled at his sister a little guiltily. 'I don't know how to tell you this, Liza, but I'm not the art dealer you believed me to be. I have actually been working as an undercover agent for the vice squad . . . '

Liza's gasp was obvious to everyone. 'The vice squad? I don't believe it!'

Charlie nodded and went on. 'I knew Anton from when we'd done a stint together in the S.A.S. We became good friends then and he's occasionally helped me out on one or two of my more difficult missions. Charity, Mitch and Vasquez were working for a powerful group I've been trying to close down for some time. They were into drug-running and guns and things like that.'

'Drugs?' Liza's eyes opened wide with shock, 'Is that what this has all been about?'

'Trying to nail the brains behind the operation is what I've been trying to do. And when I met Elizabeth I thought I'd finally found a way to do just that.' Charlie looked at Elizabeth who blushed deeply.

'I'll explain my part in all this, Charlie.' She turned to Liza and took a deep breath. 'I met Charity Gerhardt at college in Boston. I didn't realise at first what she was really like, but I didn't have many friends at college and she seemed very nice . . . '

Anton interrupted then, his face a mask of anger.

'Oh yes — very nice! She only tried

to get you hooked on drugs!'

Elizabeth looked at her brother calmly. 'I was hooked on drugs, Anton. Charity knew of my habit and she had me delivering all manner of packages whenever I came home to visit. I was getting in deeper and deeper all the time and I began to think there was no way out for me.'

She smiled at Charlie who squeezed her hand reassuringly. 'But then I met Charlie at a concert in Boston and found myself telling him all about it.'

'I, of course, told my bosses and they put me in as an undercover agent. My job was to gain the trust of the leader of the organisation and find out who the real Mr Big was.' Charlie spoke seriously.

Elizabeth nervously twisted her fingers as she went on. 'Anton tried to keep me out of it by sending me to a nursing home, but Charity found out where I was and forced me to work for them again. The gang had set up shop in Europe by now and they needed a safe house in England to store the drugs and guns in . . . '

The light suddenly dawned for Liza. 'Hazelhurst! No wonder Anton kept warning me to stay away from it!'

He smiled at her. 'I had hoped the local superstitions might do that for me, but you're a very stubborn lady when you want to be, you know.'

Liza defended herself. 'I had no choice! I had to find Stevie's dog, didn't I?'

Anton gave a battered smile. 'Poor old William, he just lumbered into it. He was always sniffing around on the moor for rabbits and suchlike and he made them nervous in case he sniffed out the narcotics and led someone to them.'

Liza shook her head in amazement, facing Anton's sister across the table. 'Elizabeth,' she asked quietly, 'were you in Daneshaw church a few weeks ago?'

Liza's question clearly unnerved the girl, 'How did you know about that?'

'I saw you.'

Elizabeth hesitated, her pale features drawn up into a frown. 'Yes, I was in the church. Mitch forced me to take another consignment. Anton thought I was in Bermuda — I didn't tell him Charity had forced me back to do yet another delivery for her.' She trailed off miserably, lapsing into silence and twisting her hands together in her lap. 'But how did you know it was me?'

'I recognised you from your photograph.'

Anton took Liza's hand in his, looking across at Charlie and Elizabeth. 'Now you see what I was up against. After that, Liza asked me all sorts of questions and I tried every trick in the book to fob her off.' He turned to grin at Liza. 'Sherlock Holmes has nothing on your sister, Charlie.'

Liza grinned back. 'And I suppose Smithy is with the CIA?'

'No,' Anton answered quietly, 'He's with the DEA.'

'The DEA?'

'Drug Enforcement Administration. He covers the Huallaga Valley in Peru for the United States. He was merely taking a spot of leave at La Chesnaie so I put him to work when it was all going to break . . . a mere precaution.'

'But why send Stevie and I to France when it was even more hairy there than at Hazlehurst?'

'That was a mistake. It was all set up for Hazlehurst, but they moved the operation to Cap Renou when they discovered I'd sent Stevie away. They wanted him as a guarantee that I would do as I was told.' He smiled at her gently. 'I'm sorry about that. I thought you'd have been safe there.'

Liza sat back in her chair, regarding her brother and Anton closely, 'Was it a connivance between you two that I work for Anton on the manuscript? Were you this mysterious friend, Charlie?'

The two men laughed and Charlie tapped the side of his nose with his finger, 'I'm afraid I'm guilty, sis. I always knew you two were made for each other.'

Liza smiled fondly at him. 'My brother, the matchmaker.'

Much later, when Charlie and Elizabeth had gone to their hotel, Anton and Liza went upstairs. They tip-toed into Stevie's room and he stirred, raising his head off the pillow and looking at them sleepily. 'Dad, can we go home soon? I want to see William again.'

'Yes, Stevie, we'll be going home very soon.'

'And Dad . . . ' he yawned widly. 'Can Liza be my mum . . . ?'

Anton glanced quickly at Liza, saying huskily, 'Only if she would like to be.'

Tears pricked the back of her eyes as she bent to kiss Stevie's cheek softly, 'There's nothing I would like more, Stevie,' she whispered. 'I love you both very much.'

'You love William, too, don't you?'

'You know I do.'

She bent to kiss him again, tucking

the sheets around him. Then, taking her hand, Anton led her out of Stevie's bedroom and back down to the living-room.

'I love you, Liza Bancroft,' he said softly.

As Anton bent his head to kiss her, all that was feminine and instinctive rose within her, awakening to meet the sensual promise of his touch. 'And I love you, too, Anton Demegar,' she whispered throatily.

Anton's arms tightened around her as he kissed her again, saying softly against her lips, 'Then you have no option but to marry me, have you? After all, you're my responsibility from now on.'

'Am I?'

'Make no mistake about it. You, me, Stevie, and William — the folks who live on the hill.'

'Sounds wonderful.'

'Mmm, it sounds pretty good to me, too . . . Tell you what, why don't we go home tomorrow and start arranging things? I don't know about you, Liza, but I don't want to wait a minute longer to make you mine.'

Liza smiled, curling into his arms. Home. It was a lovely word.

THE END

SAVAGE PARADISE
Sheila Belshaw

For four years, Diana Hamilton had dreamed of returning to Luangwa Valley in Zambia. Now she was back — and, after a close encounter with a rhino — was receiving a lecture from a tall, khaki-clad man on the dangers of going into the bush alone!

PAST BETRAYALS
Giulia Gray

As soon as Jon realized that Julia had fallen in love with him, he broke off their relationship and returned to work in the Middle East. When Jon's best friend, Danny, proposed a marriage of friendship, Julia accepted. Then Jon returned and Julia discovered her love for him remained unchanged.

PRETTY MAIDS ALL IN A ROW
Rose Meadows

The six beautiful daughters of George III of England dreamt of handsome princes coming to claim them, but the King always found some excuse to reject proposals of marriage. This is the story of what befell the Princesses as they began to seek lovers at their father's court, leaving behind rumours of secret marriages and illegitimate children.

THE GOLDEN GIRL
Paula Lindsay

Sarah had everything — wealth, social background, great beauty and magnetic charm. Her heart was ruled by love and compassion for the less fortunate in life. Yet, when one man's happiness was at stake, she failed him — and herself.

A DREAM OF HER OWN
Barbara Best
A stranger gently kisses Sarah Danbury at her Betrothal Ball. Little does she realise that she is to meet this mysterious man again in very different circumstances.

HOSTAGE OF LOVE
Nara Lake
From the moment pretty Emma Tregear, the only child of a Van Diemen's Land magnate, met Philip Despard, she was desperately in love. Unfortunately, handsome Philip was a convict on parole.

THE ROAD TO BENDOUR
Joyce Eaglestone
Mary Mackenzie had lived a sheltered life on the family farm in Scotland. When she took a job in the city she was soon in a romantic maze from which only she could find the way out.

NEW BEGINNINGS
Ann Jennings

On the plane to his new job in a hospital in Turkey, Felix asked Harriet to put their engagement on hold, as Philippe Krir, the Director of Bodrum hospital, refused to hire 'attached' people. But, without an engagement ring, what possible excuse did Harriet have for holding Philippe at bay?

THE CAPTAIN'S LADY
Rachelle Edwards

1820: When Lianne Vernon becomes governess at Elswick Manor, she finds her young pupil is given to strange imaginings and that her employer, Captain Gideon Lang, is the most enigmatic man she has ever encountered. Soon Lianne begins to fear for her pupil's safety.